MOVIE NIGHT MADNESS
FIREFLY JUNCTION COZY MYSTERY
BOOK SEVENTEEN

LONDON LOVETT

WILD FOX PRESS

Movie Night Madness

Copyright © 2023 by London Lovett

All rights reserved.

No part of this book may be reproduced in any form or by any electronic or mechanical means, including information storage and retrieval systems, without written permission from the author, except for the use of brief quotations in a book review.

ISBN: 9798853947078

Imprint: Independently published

CHAPTER 1

"Jax, I could use your help," I called out the back door. Somehow, I'd brilliantly (yes, sarcasm) come up with the idea to hold a barn raising party. We were only at the barn planning stages. There would be no jovial gathering of neighbors to help us build the thing, especially considering we hadn't ordered one piece of lumber yet. The actual raising of the barn was at least half a year off, but Jackson, my boyfriend and future farm mate, had finally picked the plans, a traditional gambrel roof barn that would eventually be painted the traditional red and white. After looking at thousands of images of barns across the country and the world, we both kept coming back to the gambrel style. Nothing said country living like a traditional red barn.

Jackson and my highly-skilled brother-in-law, Nick, had spent the last few days clearing the land and measuring and marking corner spots with stakes and flags. They were so excited about getting the rudimentary measurements and markers placed that I decided we needed to celebrate their progress. Unfortunately, having a celebration also meant preparing food and drinks. I was much better at coming up with *brilliant* plans than I was at executing them. My sisters, Lana and Emily, were far better at the hostess gig. They both insisted on bringing dishes, not so much out of generosity as from worry that I'd do a shabby job of it. I should've been insulted, only they were probably right to worry.

The back door opened and shut. One tall, dust-covered man and two equally dusty dogs came lumbering inside.

"If you guys could figure out a way to leave more of the yard outside that would be appreciated," I said tersely. I wasn't mad at Jackson or the two very dirty dogs. I was mad at the tray of mini quiches that had just come out of the oven. They'd all sunk in the middle, and they were burned around the edges. It was Emily's recipe, of course, but hers always looked like perfect golden domes. Mine were sad little puddles.

Jackson pounded his shoes on the rubber mat in front of the door. "Sunni, I was thinking—I'm going to need a place to take off my boots. Otherwise, I'll be tracking a lot more than yard into the house."

"We can talk about that later," I said curtly, then took a deep breath. "Sorry, I'm cranky because my food looks like something —like something—" I surveyed the tray of chocolate and peanut butter cookies, also slightly overdone and none of them the soft pillows of confectionary delight that Emily always produced. "Well, like something that *I* made."

Jackson smiled. (His smile always helped.) "Everything looks delicious." (The white lies helped too.) He strolled over and hugged me. He'd brought a layer of dust into the embrace, but I wasn't going to complain because I'd needed the hug.

"This is a kitchen. Not a bordello," Edward said offhandedly. He was still glued to my computer screen. I'd found my laptop quite helpful when I needed to keep my energetic and ever-present ghost occupied.

Jackson gave me a questioning look. "What's he watching?"

I motioned for Jackson to turn away from Edward and lowered my voice. "It's a little Mommy trick. You know how our parents used to turn on cartoons or a Disney movie and they told us it was so *we* could have a break and rest, but it was actually so *they* could have a break and rest?"

"Sure do. *Power Rangers* were my official babysitters after I'd stood on my mom's last nerve."

"Exactly." I lowered my voice even more. Our heads were dipped together. "Well, when I need a break from a certain ghost, I turn on the computer."

"You're not going to tell me that Gramps is watching *Little Mermaid*." Jackson glanced over his shoulder. Edward was still staring at the monitor.

"Nope. He's watching vintage Stevie Nicks music videos. He has a big crush on her."

"May I remind you that I walk through walls," Edward drawled without looking away from the screen. "You could be standing on the top floor at the end of the hallway, and I'd still hear you."

Jackson shook his head. "Creepy thing to know," he said to me pointedly. "He can hear us no matter where we are." He added another pointed look.

I shrugged sheepishly. "What can I say? He came with the house." It was little consolation, but I didn't have a solution. We had no privacy at Cider Ridge. While Edward never came down the hallway to what he considered 'my private chambers,' there was no denying that his presence was everywhere. Jackson and I were never truly alone.

"And Edward Beckett is not someone who has *crushes*," Edward continued, even after hearing the awkward turn in conversation.

"All right, an infatuation," I said sharply.

3

"No infatuations, no crushes, no banal demonstrations of passion—" He looked directly at Jackson on that phrase.

"Cool your jets, Gramps. We've all had a thing for Stevie at one time or another. You're just a little old and dead, so that makes it weird." That was Jackson getting back at Edward for the earlier comment. The insults were about to be lobbed back and forth across the kitchen like a volleyball, so I stepped in to cut the game short.

"Nope, not today. I've got guests coming. Jackson, I need you to carry the plates and silverware out to the table. And you—" I headed toward Edward. "I don't think you've seen Stevie singing 'Sara' on stage." I quickly pulled up the video and hit play.

"Yes, I've seen this. She's wearing those strange shoes."

I lifted my hand over the keyboard to find another video.

"No, this one is fine. Leave it."

Jackson was shaking his head as he carried the tray with the plates and silverware out to the table. The front door opened as the back door snapped shut. The dogs, Redford and Newman, left a trail of dust as they loped off to greet Lana and Raine.

I followed them to the entry. Lana handed me a bowl of her spinach dip, so she could greet the dogs properly. Raine, my best friend and local psychic, rushed past without a word. She was hoping to snatch a quick visit with Edward while my sister was occupied with the dogs.

Lana patted Redford. "You gorgeous man." She laughed. "Such an appropriate name for him." She lifted the pink cap she was wearing and brushed a few stray hairs back before replacing it. It was late summer, but the sun was still strong in the evening. I'd advised everyone to wear hats and sunglasses because even though we were technically eating *inside* the barn, there was no actual barn to protect us from the elements. "Sorry we're late. I had to wait for Rupert Madison's assistant to deliver the candy bars he had specially made for movie night." Lana rolled her eyes. She ran a thriving party-planning business, but she always made time to help with community projects. "If that man's ego grows any bigger, there won't be room for the rest of us on the planet."

"Rupert Madison," I repeated. "He's that big shot developer who is trying to build a shopping center off Kent Road."

"That's him. It'll happen. That man barrels through landscape with his housing developments and shopping centers like a category 5 tornado."

We headed toward the kitchen, but I kept the pace slow so Raine would have a few more seconds alone with Edward. Aside from Jackson, Raine was the only other person who knew Edward existed. In the short time she'd known him (if that's what it could be called) she'd fallen head over heels in love with him. And that was not an exaggeration. Even though Edward was mostly arrogant and even cold to her, she grew starry-eyed in his presence. I was likening it to that guy you had a big crush on in high school, and his utter indifference only made him that much more appealing. We were all gluttons for punishment, it seemed. For obvious reasons, Raine's infatuation with Edward was even more nonsensical than a shy, awkward wallflower pining over the most popular boy in school because Edward Beckett was out of bounds, literally.

Raine sealed her mouth shut as we stepped into the kitchen. Edward was still occupied with the video.

Lana stopped right in front of the computer and directly in the middle of Edward's image. Raine gasped quietly. For a brief, surreal moment in time, my sister was wearing a nineteenth century waistcoat, and Edward was wearing a pink cap.

Edward snapped back angrily. "How rude," he snarled before vanishing.

"I love Fleetwood Mac," Lana said. Her brows furrowed, and she shook her body slightly. "Is it a little cold in here?"

Raine covered her mouth to muffle a snicker.

I ignored the question. "Raine, could you carry the tray of quiches out to the yard. Jackson has a buffet table set up. Lana and I will be right behind with everything else. Em and Nick should be here soon."

Raine looked down at the tray. "Are these the quiches?"

This time it was Lana's turn to stifle a snicker.

"Yes," I said haughtily, "those are quiches."

Raine worked hard to hold back a smile as she carried the tray out to the invisible barn.

Lana and I got to work arranging fruit and freshly cut veggies on platters. "You never said—how are you involved with Madison's candy bars and movie night?"

"He ended up being the biggest donor to the end-of-summer fair and movie night, so the city council told him he could add his personalized candy bars to the movie treat bags. I'm in charge of those this year. I've got to fill two hundred treat bags for Tuesday night's big event."

"I love the end-of-summer fair and movie. Which movie did they pick this year?" I placed peach slices in a row on the platter. Emily's peach trees had been picked nearly clean. I was going to miss them. Fortunately, Emily canned some of her fruit to be enjoyed in the dead of a frosty winter.

"I guess I forgot to tell you." Lana was placing carrot sticks in a flower pattern on the tray. "They chose *Butch Cassidy and the Sundance Kid*."

"Great! Did you hear that, Redford and Newman, you're going to be on the big screen on movie night." Neither dog lifted its head. "I haven't seen that movie in a long time. Jackson will be happy to hear it. He loves that one." I stepped back from my fruit platter. It looked amateurish compared to Lana's artistically designed vegetable platter.

I sighed dejectedly. "Why didn't I get even an ounce of the hostess gene when both my sisters are Martha Stewart clones?"

Lana reached over and put her arm around my shoulder for a hug. "Because, while you were outside running around playing football and baseball with the boys in the neighborhood, Emily and I were inside learning how to be mini-Marthas. Besides, I couldn't write my way out of a paper bag."

"But Emily can," I complained. "Her blog posts put my newspaper articles to shame, and I went to school for it."

Lana lowered her arm and patted my back. "Yes, but as we both know, Emily came from another planet where everyone is born beautiful and perfect and talented."

"Wish Mom had visited that planet before she had me," I muttered as we picked up the trays to carry outside.

CHAPTER 2

The barn dinner, sans the actual barn, had been a great success. Even my quiches were eaten. We'd finished the meal with one of Emily's strawberry cheesecakes, and everyone went home complaining about being too full. Coco and Sassy, our two goats and the first inhabitants of our future farm, nibbled on carrot sticks as they hopped around what would eventually be their future barn.

Jackson carried in the last tray. He looked weary but content and very suntanned. "You should have put on more sunblock," I noted as I dried the dishes. "Three days out in the yard under that hot sun has made you look like a true farmer. No complaints here, except I don't want you to look leathery like my old softball coach, Mr. Melville."

"I don't know, I think I'd look good in leather," Jackson quipped. "What should I do with the leftover fruit and veggies?"

"Wrap them up and put them in the refrigerator." I turned back to the sink. The cleanup after a party was always one of the pitfalls that kept me from throwing more celebrations. But this one had been worth it. We'd had a great time, and it was a nice way to close out summer. The local schools opened next Monday, and the town always held a big all-day fair and carnival event the week before. The day's festivities ended with an early evening movie for the little ones. The second feature was for the adults. Everyone looked forward to it.

Jackson finished wrapping up the leftovers, then sat down at the table with a cookie. He had a bottomless stomach. I'd never heard him utter the phrase *I'm full.* "Guess I'll head home tonight. I need to wash clothes and get ready for work. It sure has been nice having a second detective on the force. Even if Detective Willow is a little ridiculous."

I glanced over my shoulder as I dried off a cookie sheet. "But he's so sweet. Talkative yes, but kind."

"He is all those things and more," he added wryly. "He's a pretty good detective, so no complaints. Now, if I had to partner with the guy, then I might lose my mind." Jackson yawned. "It's been a nice couple of days off."

"Even though you spent all of your time off on the back of a rented tractor?"

"You kidding? That was the best part. I'm going to start saving for a tractor of my own. Can't have a farm without a tractor."

I laughed. "Except we aren't planning on planting anything. What will you use it for?"

He finished the last bite of cookie. "Don't know. Just tractor-y things, I guess. I've found I have a talent for moving dirt around."

Edward scoffed from somewhere in the room. "And that rounds out the entire list of talents."

"At least I have *that* talent," Jackson sat up straighter. "You can't even stay in one piece if a breeze comes through the kitchen. The other day, the dogs pushed open the door, and your head was floating around for a good minute before it joined the rest of you."

"No more," I snapped. "It's been a long day." I was exhausted, and while it was fun having a dinner outside, the heat and the sun and the occasional unexpected breeze that caused all of us to jump up and grab runaway napkins and plates had worn me out.

"Yeah, no more," Jackson grumbled. He went to the bedroom and grabbed his things.

"Jax, I'm sorry. I'm tired and cranky. I didn't want to hear you two get into it again."

Jackson stopped and looked at me. He'd been hurt by my scolding. If I thought about it, I hated that I had acted like an angry parent. There were lots of books written about raising children, but, as far as I knew, there were no advice books on bringing up ghosts. Sometimes that was how it felt.

"You know every relationship has obstacles to deal with," Jackson said, "but ours is bigger than most. We've talked more than once about moving in together—"

"Before you're married?" Edward asked in a fair impersonation of a prim and proper Victorian matriarch.

"None of your business," Jackson and I both barked at him in unison.

Jackson took a deep breath, and his shoulders relaxed. "I want this, Sunni. I want what we have. The two of us, together forever, with a farm out back and this amazing house, but I worry it's all coming with too big of a price."

It felt as if someone had shot a cannonball at me, and it landed directly in my gut. "What are you saying, Jax?" After the fun party and laughter, this conversation was prickly and ugly.

He raked his fingers through his thick hair. "I don't know, Bluebird." Hearing my nickname in such a sad tone caused my whole chest to tighten. "I'm not sure how we're going to make this work."

"Can't you ignore him?" I asked. "I do it all the time. Just pretend he's not there."

"That's easier for you because he doesn't hurl constant insults at you. I feel like I'm in a never-ending competition with him."

"I'm right here. Remember, I can hear you from every corner of the house," Edward reminded us, unhelpfully.

Jackson looked at me with a semi-pleading look. "We've got an elephant in the room—"

"I may hear well, but my ears are not big. They're perfectly proportioned to my head," Edward added. He was never terribly astute when it came to idioms. It was hard not to feel sorry for Edward, as well. I'd been his only friend and contact after a long stretch of lonely eternity, and I liked having him around. At least, when it was just the two of us. His presence was far more stressful when I had visitors.

"Most people eventually spot the elephant and deal with it, but ours is permanent," Jackson continued. "I'm wondering how we live around it." He headed toward the front door.

I followed behind. My heart split a little with each urgent footstep. Jackson opened the door and walked out without a kiss and without looking back. I dashed out onto the porch. Adrenaline thumped through me. I leaned over the railing. "If you really want this and you really want me, then you'll find a way to deal with our elephant."

Jackson stopped before getting in his car. His amber eyes were glittering with pain. He nodded weakly before getting in the car.

"I don't understand—was this about an actual elephant?" Edward asked.

I grunted in frustration and slammed the front door behind me. The mess in the kitchen could wait. It seemed I was due for a good, long cry. I raced to my bedroom, shut the door and flopped face first onto my bed.

CHAPTER 3

I parked the Jeep down the block from the newsroom but didn't get out. I needed a few more minutes of solitude to gather my thoughts and my wits, not necessarily in that order. I'd dragged around all morning as if I had cement blocks attached to my feet. I forgot to turn on the coffeepot and, at the same time, I forgot that the toaster had recently taken on a mind of its own and if I didn't keep an eye on it, it either popped up entirely untoasted bread or a slice of charcoal. This morning it had gone the charcoal route. The entire kitchen smelled of burnt toast, and there was no rich, invigorating coffee smell to counter it.

I hardly spoke to Edward all morning even though he was being especially clingy. He knew something had transpired last night, but being a ghost, not of this world or century and, most importantly, being utterly self-absorbed, he couldn't understand what happened. I was none of those things (maybe occasionally self-absorbed but then who wasn't) and I couldn't quite understand it either. I'd never seen Jackson so upset and so unsure about our relationship. He'd been dealing with Edward and his annoying antics for well over a year, but he couldn't seem to get the rhythm of living with a ghost. It was hard to blame him. It had taken me a long time, too. Having an incorporeal being with a very large, opinionated personality was not something most couples had to deal with. Or maybe this happened more than I realized. If so, then I wished someone would publish that handbook already because I really needed it.

Lauren's pretty, fresh-washed face peered in my passenger window. She was my coworker at the newspaper. She was hired with no journalistic experience, but she'd proven to be a natural. She knocked lightly on the glass in case I hadn't seen her, even if she was a hard person to miss. She was like a human rainbow, full of color and light. You couldn't help but smile when you saw her.

My moment of reflection was over. It had been a waste of time because I was still feeling as if someone had strapped cement to my feet. With any luck, Prudence had brought in a big box of cheese Danish. Pastries wouldn't erase the heartache and confusion, but they wouldn't hurt either.

"Morning," Lauren said. Even her greeting sounded like a chorus of sweet little songbirds.

"Morning." I tried to work up the same lyrical energy, but I sounded more like a crow than songbirds.

Lauren was wearing a bright pink t-shirt that was almost too neon to look at without some kind of eye protection. It was also a color only she could pull off. I would have looked like a pink highlighter in the same shirt.

We walked together to the newsroom. "Did you have a good weekend?" She sucked in an excited breath. "How was the barn party?" She laughed. "I just love that you threw a barn party in the place where your future barn is going to be built."

The last thing I wanted to talk about was my weekend. It had started out wonderfully. Aside from my disappointing quiches, I'd considered the night a big success. But the last chapter was so heartbreaking it wiped out all the good chapters. However, Lauren's expression was filled with anticipation, so I forged ahead.

"It was wonderful. Everyone had a good time. Even Sassy and Coco. How was your weekend?"

"It was sort of a drag." Lauren opened the door. "I'd somehow managed to line up two dates for Saturday night. It was stressful trying to decide which date to keep."

Myrna looked up from the pastries she was arranging on Prue's silver platter. "We should all have such problems." Myrna ran the newspaper office and I couldn't imagine the place without her. We'd become close friends, and I always looked forward to seeing her.

"It was quite the dilemma." Lauren paused in the middle of the newsroom. The pink shirt stood out like an explosion of color in the dingy room. Parker, the editor, squinted and glanced furtively at the sunglasses on his desk.

"Hudson has five hundred thousand followers, and he has three major sponsors. Zander has three different YouTube Channels. Each one has a hundred thousand followers, and he has four big advertising deals. The choice was nearly impossible."

Myrna looked at me. "I can remember the days when you had to decide between a boy named Mark, who had his own truck, and a boy named James, who was six-foot-two."

It was rare for Parker, the editor and all-around office grump, to laugh out loud, but Myrna's comment had tickled him. I put up a good front with a jolly laugh, but inside, there was too much heartache going on to let me really enjoy the moment.

"Well, Lauren, don't keep us in suspense," Myrna said. "Who did you choose?"

Lauren sighed dramatically. "The whole thing gave me a terrible headache, so I cancelled both dates and stayed home." It was a fairly anticlimactic ending to the big date conundrum.

I put my things away and walked over to the treats. Myrna had just finished with the tray. "Everything all right, Sunni?" she asked. Myrna was always expert at sensing when I was in a glum mood. Today, that didn't take much expertise.

I picked up the biggest Danish and put it on a napkin. "I'll be fine, Myrna. Just feeling a little rough and ragged this morning. Nothing a cheese Danish and cup of coffee won't cure." I was determined to internalize that prediction too. It was the start of a new work week, and I had a job to do. I was sure the trouble between Jackson and me would work itself out. I'd never been one to mope or feel sorry for myself when it came to men, and I wasn't going to start now. In fact, when I really thought about it, this whole thing was in Jackson's court. Like I'd told him as he got in the car, if he cared enough about me, he'd find a way to deal with it.

Prudence came out of her office on a pair of sky-blue pumps. Seeing her helped me refocus on my day. She tapped her clipboard to get our attention even though she already had it. (It was a small newsroom and a small staff.)

"Morning, team," she said with vigor. "Another week of news and events is upon us."

I secretly crossed my fingers. The last thing I needed this morning was a frilly assignment, like covering the grand opening of a new cigar and pipe shop or the installation of new benches at the park. I needed something I could dig my journalistic teeth into.

"First of all, we have the end-of-summer fair and movie." Prudence always had a habit of reading down the paper as if there was a long list of newsworthy topics and reporters to go with them. It was easy to count the number of reporters in the room.

Prue looked up over her rhinestone-framed glasses. "Lauren, you'll be covering the event."

Lauren clapped quickly. She never minded any assignment. I, on the other hand, was far pickier. I breathed a mental sigh of relief at not getting the fair and movie event. Unless the second story on her list had to do with some eccentric woman's massive dollhouse collection or the new stained glass windows in the local church, I'd gotten lucky.

"Sunni." Prue returned to her list. "Let's see." It took her a moment to find my name. There were only two on the list, and she'd already covered one name. "That's right." She looked up. "I have an important and somewhat controversial assignment. I hope you're up to the task." She lifted her glasses off her face completely and gave me a scrutinizing look of concern. "Are you all right? You look a little tired."

"I'm fine." I lifted my cup of coffee. "Forgot to have my coffee before I left the house. Filling the tank now so I'll be ready to go."

Lauren laughed. "That's a good one. Mind if I use it on my blog?"

"Not at all," I said. "What's this controversial story?" I hoped it wasn't about whether the woman's club should wear yellow or pink hats to their next social event.

Prudence accepted my coffee excuse and returned her glasses to her face. "I don't know if you've been following the court case between the farmer—" She looked at her list again "—Mr. Robert Higgins, and the wealthy, well-known developer Rupert Madison—" She looked up.

"I've heard there was a legal fight about the land around Mr. Higgins' farm."

"Exactly," Prue continued. "Higgins has sued to stop Madison's latest project, the Madison Shopping Center, from being built because he insists it will impact his farm. The case will be decided today, this morning, possibly. You'll want to hurry to the courthouse, so you can be there when the decision is announced."

It wasn't exactly what I'd hoped for, but it was better than a lot of the stories Prudence had handed me.

Prudence put on her self-important expression and ran her finger down the paper on her clipboard, then she smiled. "That's all. Meeting adjourned. Now get out there and get those stories. Parker, I need to see you about this week's layout." She spun on her blue, pointy heels and disappeared into her office.

Lauren hopped up and pulled her mini backpack onto her shoulder. "I was hoping I'd get the fair and movie. What about you, Sunni? Did you want it? I'm sure I could talk to Aunt Prudence and get it changed."

"No, it's all yours, Lauren. Thanks though. It's appreciated."

CHAPTER 4

It might have been the end of summer, at least according to the school calendar, but the heat, the sun and the humidity didn't give a hoot. The combo of all three of Mother Nature's summer arsenal made standing on a cement sidewalk, in front of a black asphalt road and a white plaster building, nothing short of torture. My dismal mood only added to the discomfort. As a kid, I could stand on a shade-free baseball diamond for hours, sun pouring down like hot liquid, and hardly break a sweat. Today, I was standing beneath the shade of a straw hat with my water flask at my side, fanning myself with my notepad, and I felt sticky from head to toe.

It was hard to know when the case would finish for the day. I'd stood out on court steps for entire days only to have the judge delay the decision for another week. Protesters, mostly on Farmer Higgins' side, according to the signs, took turns chanting "Stop Madison's shopping center" from the bottom of the steps. The sweltering temperatures eventually sapped their energy. After an hour or so, they'd shortened it to "Stop Madison." Signs that had been hoisted up and down in an impressively choreographed protest march, now hung from limp wrists or had been transformed into shady shelters.

I checked my phone at least four times during my stakeout on the court steps. Not a word from Jackson. I reminded myself he was busy at work, but he usually texted me intermittently during the day to tell me some crazy or funny anecdote from his day at work or to see how my day was going. During my long, sticky morning in the hot sun, I worked hard to try and see all of it from Jackson's point of view. My parents taught us to always look at the world through someone else's eyes. Empathy was the glue that held together humanity, my mom would tell us. From Jackson's size-twelve shoes, I could see how annoying it would be to have Edward comment on everything I said and did. Nothing was off-limits, from the way Jackson combed his hair to the way he did his job. Jackson was right. It was a constant competition, the testosterone Olympics, only one of the contestants never ran out of energy or unkind remarks.

The protestors, who had mostly wilted into a group of women and men sipping greedily at their water bottles in between the occasional listless chants, had suddenly gained more energy. Signs were being lowered from their shade cloth status and were once again bobbing up and down with spirit.

The front doors of the courthouse opened. A sixty-plus man with a ruddy complexion, thinning white hair and an ill-fitting suit marched out first. His hands were rolled into angry fists. He wore an expression to match.

The protestors' newly found energy waned again, but this time it wasn't the heat. I easily concluded that the man tromping down the steps with heavy feet was the farmer, Robert Higgins. It seemed, as was so often the case, that money and power had won the day.

I rushed forward to be the first to meet him at the bottom of the steps. One of the protestors called out. "What happened, Higgins?"

"What do you think?" Higgins growled. The protestors groaned in defeat.

I stepped forward and held out my press pass. Higgins had bushy white brows. They danced up and down as he read my pass. "The *Junction Times*? Print this in your paper. Rupert Madison is a crook and a cheat and if no one stops him, he'll soon have this whole, beautiful countryside paved with cement, cheap tract homes and shopping centers. That's all I have to say." He took a step and pointed at my press pass. "You can quote me on that."

Higgins pushed forward and marched toward the parking lot, not even taking time to talk to the protestors who'd stood out in the hot sun all morning to support him.

Those same protestors picked up their signs again and started chanting "Stop Madison" with more vigor than I'd heard all morning. Sure enough, the next person to emerge from the courthouse was Rupert Madison. I'd never met him in person, but he purchased a lot of advertisement space in the paper. Every ad had a photo of Rupert Madison standing next to a sign for his latest housing development.

The chants grew louder, so loud it took me a second to notice that they'd changed the lyrics. The newest chant was "fix our homes." Two men in fancy suits with briefcases and shiny black loafers flanked Madison as he went down the steps.

The protestors moved to block the bottom step. Madison stopped halfway down. He was wearing what looked to be a designer suit. It seemed a tailor had customized it for his rather pillowy physique. His brown hair was parted down the middle and combed with gel. His massive platinum watch caught the sunlight as he motioned to one of his lawyers. The two men spoke briefly. The lawyer pulled out a phone, made a quick call and then the three men waited. Seconds later, two police guards from the courthouse came to clear the protestors back from the steps.

In my career, I'd learned right from the start, you couldn't get a story without being pushy or gutsy. So far, one quote from Higgins was all I had. As the protestors moved back, I moved forward. I flashed my press pass at one of the officers. He nodded reluctantly and let me through.

I held tightly to the pass as I reached the men on the steps. "Sunni Taylor of the *Junction Times*."

Madison remained a step higher. I assumed this was on purpose, so I had to stare up at him. "Gentlemen, thank you again, and we'll talk later." The two lawyers headed off. "Now, Miss Taylor, right?"

"Yes."

"What can I do for you? I'm a big supporter of the *Junction Times*. I spend a great deal of money on advertisements. Parker Seymour and I still meet for lunch occasionally. How is he doing?"

The man was definitely a slick salesman. I was there to interview him, and he'd already reminded me how his money supported the paper and therefore my job. On top of that, he'd tossed out the first question.

"Parker is fine. Mr. Higgins didn't have much to say about the case."

He grinned. "I'm sure he didn't." A chuckle followed.

"I assume that means you won the case."

"Judge nearly laughed Higgins out of the courtroom. Poor man didn't have a case at all. The land I own, the land I plan to develop into a magnificent shopping center, does not affect his farm at all."

"So, building the shopping center won't impact him with noise or the inconvenience of large trucks driving past his farm?

The Higgins Farm is out on Kent Road. It's very remote and doesn't get much traffic. Surely, you can see how this might impact Mr. Higgins even if the shopping center is not directly on his land." My journalistic integrity always somehow landed me on the side of the underdog. I'd keep the writing unbiased, naturally. But it was always hard not to stick up for the little guy when facing down someone pompous and powerful like Madison.

Madison's gaze flickered with annoyance. It was obvious he was a man who rarely got questioned about anything. "Progress can't happen without a little noise and dust. Eventually, the center will be finished and—"

"And there'll be even more traffic going that direction," I added.

"With any luck," he said. I half expected him to lick his thin lips with greed. "Now, if you'll excuse me, I have a shopping center to plan." He pushed past me.

"Do you think we need a shopping center?" I called to his back. "There are at least three centers within a ten-mile radius with vacant storefronts." My comment drew a round of applause from the protestors, but Madison never looked back.

CHAPTER 5

A woman, forty-something, tanned, in workout shorts and holding a sign that read "Madison is a crook" headed my direction. She reached me on the steps. "That was brilliant." She glanced at the press pass hanging around my neck. "*Junction Times*, Sunni Taylor," she read. She took off her sunglasses and hooked them on the collar of her shirt. "I'm Veronica Blaine. You wrote that great piece exposing the corrupt connection between the city planner and the city council. Kudos to you. Not every journalist, especially local ones, are willing to stick their necks out like that."

"Thank you. I appreciate that. I noticed your group switched their chant. Something about fix our homes?"

Veronica realized the sun on the bleached white steps was too bright. She put her sunglasses back on. "That's right. I'm president of the Ridgemont Homeowners' Association. Our neighborhood of forty homes is off Fielding Avenue. It was a Madison development." She shook her head. "Worst decision of my life. Don't get me wrong. I love my neighbors and community. The homes are only three years old, and we've been dealing with nonstop problems. All because Madison cut corners and paid off city inspectors."

I had my notebook in hand but hadn't written anything down yet. "Do you mind if I use your name and this information in my article?"

"Not at all. Please do," she added enthusiastically. "Anything to expose that greedy man and his never-ending corruption."

"You mentioned that he paid off city inspectors. That's a very bold charge. Do you have any proof to back it up? Otherwise, I can't print it."

She fidgeted with her sunglasses. "Proof? Well, I don't have receipts or secret recordings, if that's what you mean. But the contractor in charge of the Ridgemont development told me Madison was constantly asking him to cut corners and violate codes. How else did the houses pass inspection without some palm greasing?"

It made sense. However, I wasn't stepping into that sticky mess without actual proof. "You've kept in touch with the contractor? What's his name?"

More fidgeting. Veronica hesitated about giving out the name.

"I could talk to the contractor and get him to corroborate what you told me. Then I'd have something more solid to report on," I noted.

"Oh, you won't get anything from Curtis Lang. As much as he hated working for Madison, I've heard he's trying to land the contract for the new shopping center."

I wrote the name down anyhow.

"Don't tell him I told you all this," she said, solidifying my decision not to use any of Veronica's quotes in my article.

"I must say, I'm rather surprised a contractor would tell you about the corner cutting. Were you two friends?"

She laughed. "Heavens, no. We'd been having so many

problems, and I'm not talking about cracks in the driveways or a loose roof tile. Although, those problems have come up too. Some of the homeowners have had nonstop plumbing problems. Sewage backing up into showers, toilets not properly installed, kitchen sinks with terrible water pressure. And don't get me started on the electrical. One day—" she said, obviously getting started "—the entire neighborhood went black. Everyone lost power. The utility company said it was faulty wiring at the main transformer. It's just one thing after another, which is why the HOA is suing both Lang and Madison. When we started filing all the complaints, Madison handed off the problems to Lang. After letting them both know we were hiring a lawyer, Curtis agreed to come to one of our meetings." She chuckled. "Boy, did we let him have it. I thought the poor man was going to crawl out the back door to escape the ruckus. That was when he told us that he was constantly ordered to cut corners. He said Madison told him not to worry about the inspections because he would take care of it. He even used air quotes as he said it."

"It sounds as if I should talk to Lang. He basically told everyone at the HOA that Madison forced him to ignore building codes. That's a pretty big accusation. I should get his side of the story."

Veronica's smile faded as I spoke. "That's just it. The HOA meeting was six months ago. Once Madison started collecting bids for a big shopping center, Lang zipped up fast. He's now denying that he ever said such things. He wants that lucrative contract. Money over integrity."

"Veronica, some of us need to get out of this hot sun. We're going to head back home," one of the protestors called.

"All right. Thanks for your help. I'll send out an email about the next meeting. I'll provide sandwiches and post a sign-up list on the corkboard in the recreation room for the rest of the lunch.

Terry, if you could bring those delicious brownies, that would be great. They're a good mood booster."

A woman, Terry, I assumed, smiled and nodded. The hot, tired and mostly dejected group picked up their signs and their water bottles and tromped, with heavy feet, toward the parking lot.

"What can you include in your article?" Veronica asked.

"I can certainly talk about the issues you and your neighbors are having with the houses you bought." I always kept a few business cards with my contact information tucked in the plastic sleeve of my press pass. I pulled one free. "Email me at the newspaper. Send a list, specific as you can, of some of the more significant problems. This isn't the first time I've heard about Madison's housing developments being shabbily built. Of course, I'll have to get his side of the story too. I'm interested to see what he says about it. He certainly cut me off when I started asking him uncomfortable questions about the shopping center's impact on the Higgins Farm."

Veronica tucked the card into her pocket and reached for her sign. "I'll send you that list right away. Anything we can do to expose Rupert Madison as a scam artist will be a win for our community."

"No promises. As you saw today from this court case, Madison has the money and power to stay on top. I'll certainly bring up the problems your association is having. If nothing else, maybe he'll be shamed into doing something about it."

A dry laugh shot from her mouth. "He won't budge. Like you said, he has the money and power to get away with it, and frankly, he's despicable. I'll type up that list when I get home. You should see it in your email in the next few days. I'll have to canvas the neighborhood to get more specifics."

Like her protest partners, I was just as anxious to get out of the sun and heat. "I'll keep an eye out for it. Nice meeting you." I gulped the rest of my water as I walked back to the Jeep.

The interior felt like an oven. I couldn't touch the steering wheel. I turned on the engine and blasted the air conditioner. Only warm air shot out at first. It would take a good few minutes to cool down and even longer for me to cool down.

It had been a fairly uneventful morning, and I was glad of it. Even after my internal pep talk, my heart and head were not in it today. I was also running on cheese Danish and coffee. I needed lunch, but what I needed even more was a chat with Raine. To compound my ghost and boyfriend problems, the ghost part of the equation made it impossible for me to confide and commiserate with my sisters. Not that I didn't enjoy having girl-to-girl chats with Raine. She was my best friend. But big-ticket items, like my relationship with Jackson, required sisterly advice. Since Edward was the thorn in this particular setback, I'd need to turn to Raine. She was the only person I could talk to about this unique problem. And unique it was.

I pulled out my phone and sent a text. "I could really use a shoulder to cry on today. Lunch in an hour at Layers?" If Raine was in the middle of a tarot card session or tea leaf reading she wouldn't respond right away. I was in luck. She was between clients, and she texted right back.

"Uh oh. Sounds serious. I'll see you in an hour." She added in a heart emoji, which was exactly what I needed to see.

I wrote back a half-hearted *yay*. And that's how I was feeling—half-hearted, and the half that was left wasn't feeling too great either.

CHAPTER 6

I had no idea how badly I needed a friend to lean on until I spotted Raine, smiling and waving at me from one of the picnic tables outside of Layers, a local favorite specializing in sandwiches named for old-time celebrities. My throat tightened, and I wiped away a tear as I headed toward her. It didn't take Raine's sixth sense to realize something was very off with her friend. Her smile dropped, and a look of concern crossed her face. She got up from the table and met me halfway.

"Sunni? My gosh, what's happened?"

We hugged in silence. It was what I needed to collect myself. I wiped another tear and then chided myself for letting it get that far in the first place. Seeing Raine, my good, trusted friend, caused emotions to well up inside of me, and today, I was a boiling teapot of emotions.

We ended the embrace. Raine leaned back and adjusted her glasses to get a closer look at me. "You look as if you've been through an ordeal. I'm sensing this has something to do with Jackson."

My talented best friend was always supernaturally perceptive. Especially when it came to me.

We hugged again briefly. "Let's get lunch ordered, then you can tell me all about it. My treat today, and don't say no because you know I rarely offer to pay." She added in a scolding glance to let me know there would be no argument.

If I walked inside Layers, the first thing Ballard, the owner, would ask is "how is Jackson?" I wasn't in the mood to talk about him or us. Again, Raine read my thoughts. (Sometimes, like today, her sixth sense came in handy. Other times, it bordered on unsettling.)

"I'll go order for both of us, so you don't have to answer a bunch of questions or make small talk." Raine lifted her glasses. She only did so when she was close and in a scrutinizing mood. "You look like you could use a Douglas Fairbanks. Tuna on sourdough with a pickle and iced tea on the side?"

I smiled weakly. These few minutes with her had already made me feel better. "It's like you read my mind," I quipped.

"I've been known to do that on occasion." She pushed the half dozen bangles on her thin, tanned wrist higher. Like always, they slid back down to her hand. The bangles were such a part of Raine, I wasn't sure I'd recognize her without the customary clinking of her bracelets. Her skirt was sewn from dozens of blue and white bandanas. The handmade garment fluttered in the breeze as she hurried into the restaurant to place our order.

I sat at the same table she'd been holding for us. The tulip poplars surrounding Ballard's popular restaurant provided enough shade for diners to eat outside in spring and summer. My fingers inadvertently grazed over a patch of graffiti scratched into the picnic bench. Jackson and I had sat at the outside tables enough to have memorized all the impromptu sentiments. I knew which words my fingers had touched before I looked down at them. "Henry loves Alana." Henry had taken the time to etch a heart around his words. We didn't know Henry and Alana, but whenever we sat at this particular table, one of us would say, "I wonder if Henry still loves Alana." It was a corny tradition, but we'd always laugh about it.

Raine returned with the cold drinks and our food order number. "Ballard wanted to know why you didn't come inside to order. I told her you'd been standing in the hot sun all morning, and you needed to sit in the shade."

I took a much-needed drink of tea. "How did you know I was in the hot sun all morning? Your sixth sense is on fire today."

"So is your face, pal. Did you put on sunblock?"

Instinctively, I touched my face. It felt hot. "Darn, I was so out of it, I forgot to put any on. Do I look like a lobster?"

"Not quite lobster. At least you were wearing a hat."

I'd left my hat in the Jeep. Before I could gush about her extraordinary skills, she put up a hand to stop me.

"You've got a white line." She ran her finger across her own forehead to illustrate.

"I must look like a clown. I was on the steps of the courthouse waiting for the Higgins versus Madison case to be decided."

"Madison won," Raine said. Again, she jumped ahead of my accolades. "It was all over town this morning while I was running errands. Some people are excited about a new shopping center. Others hate Madison and his over urbanization of everything. One of my clients is in the middle of a lawsuit against Madison. I've heard his homes are money pits."

I sat up out of my slump. The mopey posture had been with me all morning, even after I resolved not to mope. "Veronica Blaine?"

Raine was mid-sip. She pulled the straw free from her mouth. "Yes, have you met her?"

"I met her this morning at the courthouse. She was protesting with a group of disgruntled homeowners. Let's just say, she's not a big fan of Rupert Madison."

"That's the funny thing. About three years ago, after she'd signed up to purchase one of the homes in the development, Veronica started dating Rupert. She would talk to me about their relationship. She had dreams of becoming quite the socialite by eventually marrying the most successful businessman in town. After about four months, Rupert broke it off. She was devastated. However, I think the heartbreak had more to do with her missing out on that dream life of nice cars and expensive clothes than it did with Rupert no longer being part of her life."

"So, he compounded his problems by selling a less-than-quality house to a woman he broke up with. Not too smart."

Our number was called. Raine swung her legs over the bench to pick up the food. I took the few seconds alone to check my phone. No texts or messages from Jackson. Raine returned with our orders. I'd filled up with iced tea and my appetite was not as good as usual, but Raine beamed as she handed me my Douglas Fairbanks. "There you go."

She lifted her long skirt and threw her leg over the bench. We each took a few bites before she put down her sandwich, wiped her hands on a napkin and placed them in front of her on the table. "Now, what's going on? Or should I tell you?"

"Maybe it'll be easier coming from you. When I talk about it, my throat aches."

"Oh, Sunni, I'm sorry. It's the boys, isn't it?"

I squinted one eye at her. "Define boys."

"The tall, incredibly handsome solid one and the tall, incredibly handsome vaporous one."

"How did you know?" I asked.

"Well, you and Jackson get along so well. I figured it couldn't have been something amiss between you. That left your one notable and ever-present problem. Edward Beckett." Little diamonds sparkled in her eyes as she said his name, and the way she pronounced it made it sound like frosting, if frosting had a sound.

"I don't know what to do, Raine. Jackson left the house last night so hurt, so disillusioned with everything. We've both been so excited about starting our farm, but last night he was questioning whether or not living together was even possible. Edward is always there, hovering, lurking, listening in. He's especially attentive whenever Jackson is with me."

"I've told you my theory on that."

I looked up in question.

Raine rolled her eyes. "Edward is in love with you. And trust me that is not easy for this besotted ghost lover to admit. It's a competition."

"That's what Jackson called it. But there is no competition. I mean Edward is, as you pointed out, basically vapor. Granted, I enjoy his company, and we have long, meaningful conversations and debates about whether life was better back in his day or in mine. Even if we weren't good friends, it's not as if I can do anything about his presence. He's there. As permanent a fixture as the walls and roof. I've told Jackson to learn to ignore him."

"Edward is not easy to ignore," Raine noted.

"You don't have to tell me that. He's always extra arrogant and annoying when Jackson is in the house. And Jackson jumps right into the fray. They get started and, suddenly, I'm the mom figure scolding her boys, yelling at them to stop fighting. It's not a pretty look for a relationship."

Raine reached across. Her bangles jingled as she placed her hand on my arm. "Why don't you try talking to him?"

"I have. I told Jackson if he cared about me, he'd learn to ignore Edward."

Raine was shaking her head. "No, not Jackson. Talk to Edward."

I laughed but Raine wasn't laughing along. "Wait. You're serious?" I asked to make sure.

"Yes. Edward will listen. Tell him that this whole thing is breaking your heart. He loves you."

I started an eyeroll. She cut it short by squeezing my hand. "He'll pay attention. I'm sure of it." Confident she'd given solid advice, she released my hand and returned to her sandwich.

I stared down at my Douglas Fairbanks. Was Raine right? It wouldn't hurt to try. I had nothing to lose.

CHAPTER 7

With the courtroom drama over, I had spare time. I considered, for all of a minute, going home to have that talk with Edward, but I wasn't prepared. I wasn't sure how to approach the subject in a way that wouldn't offend or hurt Edward. I needed that ghost handbook to learn how not to hurt a ghost's feelings, and my ghost, in particular, was hypersensitive about everything. Edward's moods could change like the weather out on the prairie.

The tuna sandwich and heart-to-heart with Raine had helped fortify me, but not enough to face Edward. Without giving it much thought, I turned my Jeep in the direction of the summer fair. It wasn't open to the public yet, but my press pass would get me inside.

Work trucks and food vans lined the side of the road. The fair and outdoor movie theater were being set up in the middle of the town's biggest park. It was a massive common space where locals could ride bikes and walk dogs along narrow cement paths that snaked between stretches of green lawn, playing fields and shade trees. Since my house sat on what I liked to tell the dogs was their personal dog park, I rarely took them to the town's park. They had their own doggie playground out the back door. That thought reminded me of the future barn. Jackson was so excited about it. He'd been working hard to get the building site ready. Was he really willing to give up on his dream? I had to stop thinking about it or risk falling right back into the state of glumness that had weighed me down all morning.

Lauren's shiny car was parked between a city work truck and a van with a party rental logo on the side. The back doors of the van were open. A man was rolling a glossy, yellow-striped popcorn making cart down a portable ramp. Even though everyone filled up on grease and sugar-laden goodies at the fair, there was still always room for movie snacks. And it wasn't movie night without the nostalgic, familiar aroma of freshly popped popcorn. The morning after usually brought flocks of birds and packs of squirrels. They were the unofficial cleanup crew.

Classic kiddie rides, the kind I would personally never put my dog on, let alone my child, were being assembled in the center of the park that was usually used for soccer games. The outdoor theater took less work. Wooden deck chairs were being placed on the far field. A massive screen would be rolled out along with a projector. Colorful game booths were being erected around the perimeter of the sports fields. The traditional dunking booth had been pulled out of storage for its once-a-year debut. Several years ago, a local artist had spruced up the famous dunk tank by painting gold and silver fireflies on a dark blue background. Local teens, most likely the kids of the event staff, were testing out the booth. Their laughter and splashes could be heard over the general clamor of hammers and drills. They weren't bothering with throwing a ball at the paddle. Instead, they took turns sitting on the dunk seat while friends ran and hit the paddle with their fists, guaranteeing a supreme dunk.

Something that stood out as different this year were the

numerous life-sized cutouts of Rupert Madison standing in various places around the park. Lana had mentioned that he'd contributed a great deal of money to the event. Apparently, having his face smiling down at all the attendees was part of the deal. The cutout closest to where I was standing was a photo of Madison holding a small model of his future shopping mall. Notably, someone had pushed a big nail directly through his forehead.

"Sunni," Lauren's voice shot over my shoulder.

I spun around. She was walking with a woman, a member of the event staff, according to the pale yellow shirt she was wearing.

Lauren had pulled on a visor with an exceptionally large bill. It shaded most of her face. "I didn't expect to see you here this morning. Deborah, this is my mentor, Sunni Taylor. I'm sure you've read her amazing articles. Sunni, this is Deborah Jones. She's in charge of this whole affair. Can you imagine taking on such a big project?"

I'd seen Deborah before at council meetings and other town events. She'd pulled a cap down over thick, dark hair, and she was standing in a cloud of sunblock fragrance. "Sunni Taylor. I read your column every week."

I nodded humbly. "Lauren is right. This is a massive undertaking." I glanced around. "Everything seems to be going smoothly."

Deborah's mouth pulled down. "Shh, never say that out loud." She laughed lightly, but I sensed that she was worried. "I'm sorry. I'm so superstitious."

I looked around briskly for some wood, but the only thing nearby was the cardboard Rupert Madison. I knocked on his likeness three times. "Cardboard comes from wood, right?"

Lauren laughed but Deborah didn't look too convinced. I was sure if something went wrong, Deborah Jones would be cursing the day I was born. For now, at least, something else had caught her attention. She lifted the brim of her cap as she moved closer to the cardboard cutout. "Is that a nail in his forehead?" she asked.

"It was there before I—you know—said the thing I wasn't supposed to say." I wanted to make sure she knew I wasn't to blame.

Lauren found the whole exchange amusing enough that rather than lifting the enormous bill on her visor, she tugged it down to hide her smile.

Deborah wasn't nearly as tall as the cardboard Madison, so she had to stand up on tiptoes to reach the nail in his forehead. She gave it a good tug and removed the nail. As expected, it left a sizeable hole in his face. She shook her head. "Those teenagers. I'll have to replace this one. Mr. Madison will be angry if he sees it. I'm going to go to the storage room and get a new one."

"There are more?" Lauren asked, still suppressing a smile.

Deborah nodded. "At least a dozen but I ran out of room." She waved her arm around the fair. There were at least that many already standing in different locations in the park. "I thought more would start to look ridiculous." She grunted in frustration. "I have many important things to do, but I suppose I better take this cutout back to storage. If there's nothing else, Lauren, we can talk again later."

Lauren slipped her iPad into her bag. "You've been a great source for information. I'd love to talk more later when you have time. I know you're super busy."

"Nice meeting you, Miss Taylor," Deborah said.

"Same to you. Can we help you carry Mr. Madison to storage?" I asked and couldn't stop a snicker at how odd the question sounded.

"Nope, I'm fine." Deborah gripped each side of Mr. Madison's cardboard hips and yanked him out of the ground. She turned him sideways and tucked the cutout under her arm before carrying off the paper Rupert Madison like a surfer with her board.

Lauren could no longer hold back her laughter. "Oh my gosh, I'm so glad I never had a class with you. I'd get in so much trouble with the teachers for bursting out laughing. I thought I'd die when you went to knock three times on the cardboard cutout."

I winced. "I'm afraid I'm going to be blamed if anything goes wrong at this event."

"What could go wrong? It's the summer fair."

"Hey, Lauren, how's it going?" Three boys, possibly seventeen or eighteen and soaking wet from the dunking booth, had wandered over to talk to my pretty coworker.

"Kyle, how are you? How is your sister?"

Water dripped off Kyle's t-shirt, leaving a puddle around his feet. "She got a job in New York. She's leaving next week."

"Good for her. I'll have to call her."

Talking to Lauren was causing him to fidget. He shyly tucked his hands in his pockets, which was a difficult casual look to pull off when you were soaking wet. "See you around, Lauren." He realized after speaking about his sister, there was little else to discuss. He and his friends walked away awkwardly, leaving a trail of water in their wake.

"That's Kyle Lang," Lauren explained. "I went to school with his sister, Mallory. She studied fashion design."

"Lang," I repeated. "Is he related to Curtis Lang, the contractor?"

"Curtis is his dad." Lauren's eyes rounded. "I'll bet Kyle was the one who pushed that nail through the cardboard cutout."

"I thought Lang and Madison were partners on construction projects. I learned just this morning that Curtis was trying to land the contract for Madison's shopping center."

Lauren tugged the bill of her visor a little lower and moved closer. "I heard from my friend, Julie, this morning. She is friends with Mallory Lang too. In fact, they're best friends. She said that Lang Construction didn't get the contract. Madison already had someone else lined up, some out-of-state contractor who underbid everyone else by thousands. Rupert Madison is all about profits."

"Even if it means putting up an inferior shopping center," I added. "I've heard he's a big corner cutter when it comes to his buildings and houses."

"I've heard the same thing." Lauren lifted her nose and breathed in deeply. "Smells as if they've started up the cotton candy machines. I'm a sucker for blue cotton candy."

I smiled. "Cotton candy does bring with it those wondrous childhood memories. I prefer pink because it doesn't leave your teeth and tongue blue."

"That's the best part. Want to go try some? My treat."

The sugary scent reached me as she made the offer. "You know what? Why not? I might even try the blue."

CHAPTER 8

After a glorious half hour nibbling tufts of blue cotton candy and filling Lauren in on all the stuff we old people used to do in the days before cell phones and social media (I left her with the feeling that she'd missed out on a lot while being glued to her phone) I forced myself back into work mode. I'd heard some fairly scandalous charges from Veronica Blaine about Rupert's business practices. It was time to hear his side of the story. He'd cut me off short this morning, but I was sure he'd be interested in countering some of the accusations. Especially to a local reporter. A little research and a phone call to Madison's office led me to an in-progress housing development five miles outside of town.

The man certainly was doing a great deal of building. When was it considered too much? There was a housing shortage in our area, but it was hard not to worry that replacing nature with houses was going to ruin the character of our quaint community. It was a tough balancing act.

However, Rupert didn't seem to be worried about erasing the natural landscape. As I drove the Jeep along the newly laid asphalt road, the Sunridge Community housing development came into view. As was the case with most new neighborhoods, the landscape was a barren wasteland of treeless lots, new sidewalks and cement driveways. Six new houses stood shiny and new, and, if I was being frank, characterless in the midday sun. Another four were timber skeletons, all the same shape and height. Work trucks and construction workers covered the free space between housing tracts. A water truck worked its hardest, spraying water like an elephant over the dry, dusty lots. There was still plenty of residue in the air. A shiny black Cadillac with a license plate that read RMINC was parked in front of one of the finished model houses. A colorful flag with the words *Sunridge Community* waved wildly from the top of a tall flagpole. A sign mounted on posts beneath the fluttering flag boasted that Sunridge was a community of three-to-four bedroom, single family homes. The most notable thing about the emerging neighborhood was there was not one speck of green anywhere.

I gave a tug on my press pass for luck. I had no idea what kind of reception I'd get, but the woman who answered the phone at the office let me know she'd call Madison and tell him to expect a visitor.

Rupert was easy to spot because he was the only person on site not wearing work clothes. His pristine dark suit was easy to find. The only change in his attire from this morning at the courthouse was the bus-yellow hardhat on his head. He was talking to another man, a construction supervisor, I surmised, by the lack of dirt on his work clothes.

I headed straight toward them with as much confidence as I could muster. Normally, that would have been more than enough fortitude, but my courage was lacking today.

The supervisor noticed me first. He glanced my direction and said something to Madison. Rupert looked over his shoulder, then said something else back. My guess would have been "there's that pesky reporter again." His worker walked away. Madison turned toward me with a welcoming smile.

"It's you," he said with a stiff grin. "Patricia said a reporter was dropping by the site."

"Yes, it's me again. We didn't get much chance to talk this morning. You're a busy man, I know, but I thought you might want to address some comments I heard this morning." I surveyed the half-finished neighborhood we were standing in. Barren and empty as it was, it was hard to imagine it as a bustling family neighborhood. At the moment, it was merely an unfinished tapestry of concrete and timber. "It's about the quality of your homes."

His thick brows drew together. "The quality of the homes?" A cynical, smug grin appeared on his thick, round face. "You've been talking to Veronica Blaine. Did she mention that we used to date? She was clingy. I let her down easy, gave her the whole 'it's me, not you' speech, but our breakup really tore her up. Any criticism she has is purely subjective and biased."

"Except she lives in a Madison home. Correct?"

The smug grin twisted and turned into a frown. "There is nothing wrong with her home. In fact, I stand behind all my houses. Would you care for a tour of the site? You can see for yourself that we are building fine homes here at Sunridge."

My lack of knowledge about house building wasn't going to make me a great judge, but I'd lived through nearly three years of home renovation. Henry and Ursula, my contractors, took great pride in their work. If nothing else, I knew what quality craftsmanship looked like.

"I'd love a tour."

"Great." His loud whistle startled me. "Hey, Oscar, get me a hardhat, would ya?" Seconds later, a man hurried over from a truck with a yellow hardhat.

I placed it on my head and gave it a tap on top for good measure. "Lead the way, Mr. Madison."

"The model home is the only finished home in the neighborhood, but it'll give you a good idea of what the homes will look like. I can have Patricia email you the details, so you can list prices, finishes, square feet and all the important details in your article." He made it instantly clear why he was so eager to give me a tour. He was hoping for some free advertisement.

The model home had even less character inside. I was spoiled by the beauty and charm of the Cider Ridge Inn. Madison's model home was basically walls, vinyl floors and the plainest looking kitchen I'd ever seen. It was entirely void of the qualities that make four walls a home.

He showed me around. I pretended to be interested, all while formulating some questions that might prickle him into answers that would make this whole visit worthwhile.

"Miss Blaine mentioned there's a lawsuit pending. She said the HOA in her neighborhood has a long list of complaints. She's sending me specific problems. Will you consider fixing the problems to avoid a court trial?"

"Our homes have a warranty for the first year. Her neighborhood is three years old. She has no legal leg to stand on." He waved me toward the front door.

We stepped back out into the sunshine. "Feel the difference?" he asked. "Energy efficient heating and cooling in each house. There's going to be a swimming pool and community center on this next block. Let me show you."

Much like my barn, the community center and future pool were merely stakes with small red flags showing where the center and pool would eventually sit.

"We'll be adding a children's playground, and there'll even be a corner park. As you can see, I strive to create ideal, convenient communities for families."

"I can see a lot of planning goes into it, but if the houses come with plumbing and electrical problems that is hardly ideal." Lucky Mr. Madison got me on a day when I was feeling especially ornery and less than charitable, particularly toward men. My further prodding about the quality issues irritated him. His shoulders stiffened, and he tugged on the bottom of his coat. A group of workers were sitting on a portable table eating their lunches. They ate sandwiches, drank from thermoses and worked hard to pretend they weren't listening to the exchange.

"Miss Blaine is going to be sorry she spoke to the press about the lawsuit. I'll inform my lawyers she's out telling lies to journalists. We might have to add libel to our countersuit." A tiny spray of spittle flew from his mouth as he spoke. I'd pushed him one question too far.

"I'm quite busy, and I think I've given you more than enough of my time." He herded me like a lost sheep back toward the new sidewalk. As we passed the group of workers, one of the men absently tossed an apple core on the ground. The chewed-up core rolled right into our path, and Madison stepped on it. The young man, possibly late twenties with stringy dark hair and a short beard, looked positively mortified.

"Excuse me, Mr. Madison," he said nervously. "Didn't see you walking there." His apology seemed genuine. It was an instance of bad timing and physics.

Madison was already tense because of the pushy reporter. He spoke through clenched teeth. "What's your name?" he asked harshly. The young man's coworkers were ducking deep into their lunches to avoid eye contact with the boss.

The young man swallowed hard. "It's Jeremy Sexton, sir. I'll pick it up right now." He hurried over, leaned down beneath Madison's glower and picked up the dirt covered core. I'd been asking questions and getting salesman-style answers, but right there, in that moment, I was getting a true picture of Rupert

MOVIE NIGHT MADNESS

Madison's character. It was ugly. Still, I could never have anticipated what came next.

Jeremy straightened and found himself face-to-face with Madison. "Again, I apologize."

"Not accepted," Madison sneered. "Turn in your tools and your hardhat and get off the work site. You're fired."

Jeremy's bearded chin dropped nearly to his chest. Mine too. "Sir?"

"You heard me. I'll let your supervisor know. As of right now, you no longer work here."

The man's chin wobbled. He stood still, in shock, for a second. His shoulders sank as he walked back to pick up his lunch pail. His coworkers weren't going to stick around and get caught up in the mess. They ended their lunches fast. Half-eaten sandwiches were wrapped up and stuck back into lunch pails. They left a cloud of dust in their wake.

Madison wasn't *my* boss, thank goodness. "I'd say that was one of the cruelest things I've ever witnessed from a boss, and I used to work for some of the toughest, grouchiest city newspaper editors in the business." I plucked the hardhat off my head and shoved it at him. I sensed he thought it was beneath him to handle something as lowly as the return of a hardhat. "I'll see myself off the property."

"See that you do," he growled.

"Now, I can see why someone jammed a nail through your face on those ridiculous cardboard cutouts at the fair."

His jaw tightened even more. "I'll let Parker know I no longer plan to advertise in the *Junction Times*. There are plenty of other local papers that can use the revenue."

I spun around and marched purposefully back to my Jeep. I'd probably stuck my foot in it this time. Prudence would be angry with me. That was fine. It felt good to give the man a piece of my mind.

CHAPTER 9

My adrenaline was pumping after my unpleasant trip to the Sunridge Community. That was Madison's ruse—name the community something that sounded pleasant. It literally had the word sun in it. Boast about all the family-friendly amenities and people, especially young families, fell into his trap of spending hard-earned money on bad houses.

I'd heard from two sides of a story, but there was a third side to this one. The farmer, Mr. Higgins, had been too disappointed at his loss to stick around for an interview. Now that he'd had time to cool off, I thought a trip to his farm was in order. After what I witnessed at the building site, I found I had a craving to talk to Mr. Madison's enemies. It seemed he had a few.

With a short bout of research, I learned that the Higgins Farm was a hundred acres, and the land had been passed down for three generations. The farm grew corn and barley alongside a small herd of cattle. I'd seen the farm in passing, but never really gave it a scrutinizing look.

I stopped the Jeep on the road before turning onto the long, dirt drive that led up to the two-story farmhouse. It was far less charming than I envisioned for a family farm. A tractor that looked as if it had seen better days sat in front of a pile of old tractor tires. A handful of scraggly-looking chickens pecked at the ground around the tractor. I was biased when it came to chickens. Emily took such good care of hers. The girls were always plump and clean with fluffy feathers and bright eyes. Robert Higgins' chickens looked as if laying an egg would take all their energy.

I turned onto the dirt driveway. Dust kicked up around me as I rolled slowly toward the farmhouse. Shutters hung crookedly on windows, and some of the wood siding on the home was rotted and discolored. An old Ford truck was parked in front of the house. Next to it was a shiny white Tesla. Not the kind of car I expected to see at a hundred-year-old farmstead.

I parked the Jeep. As I got out, the front door opened. A woman in a business suit with a persnickety bun at the back of her head stepped out first. She was holding a briefcase. She turned to shake Robert's hand, then stepped carefully down the rickety front steps on her pointy heels.

Higgins spotted my Jeep before he shut the door. He stepped onto the front porch and crossed his arms. I was hoping for more gracious body language, but that didn't stop me from walking toward the house. The Tesla rolled away, in its electrical silence and a cloud of dust.

"Mr. Higgins." I had my pass ready.

He lowered his arms when he got a better look at me. "You're the reporter from the courthouse."

"Yes, I hope you don't mind me showing up at the farm." Before he could say he did mind, I forged ahead. "I had an interview with Madison, and I wanted you to have equal time to tell your story."

My diplomacy worked. His stance and suspicious glower softened. "Unfortunately, there's not much to say." He motioned for us to move beneath the shade of a massive maple tree. The chickens joined us, certain our pockets were filled with scratch or mealworms. "Madison has the money and power to get everything he wants. That, in turn, makes him wealthier and more powerful. It's a vicious cycle. Not one a humble farmer like me can break." He motioned toward the Tesla that was turning onto the road. "That was a realtor. I've decided to sell the farm."

"But it's been in your family for three generations."

He seemed pleased that I'd done my research. "That's right. My son lives in Seattle with his wife and children. He doesn't want to run this place. It doesn't make enough money anymore." He shook his head slowly. "Money and power saw to that, too. Corporate farms have all but wiped us little guys out. I don't need much. I'm able to pay the bills and keep the creditors away. However, it's not enough for a family."

"What a shame," I said. "This is your life. You're going to have to move and turn it upside down."

"It won't be too bad. I'm going to move to Seattle, be near my grandkids." He looked up toward a distant pasture. A dozen cows stood grazing under the hot, late-afternoon sun. "I already have a buyer for my herd. Just not sure who wants an old farm these days."

I smiled. "I'm working on building up a farm myself. I live in the Cider Ridge Inn. My boyfriend and I are going to build a barn soon." As I said it, my heart sank. What if that never happened? Were the farm dreams disappearing along with our relationship? I had to shake myself out of my thoughts. I was on assignment.

"The Cider Ridge? Beautiful old home. Lucky you. I wish you well with your plans. The Cider Ridge is on a quiet piece of land that can't be intruded upon by greedy developers." He was right. My sisters and I were lucky. The entire piece of land with the three farms had been handed down to our mom in a trust.

There was no place for a shopping center or busy road or pop-up family community.

"I'm very sorry this happened to you, Mr. Higgins. You gave me a quote earlier. Is there anything else you'd like to add?" I pulled out my notebook.

"Just this. When is it enough? How many shopping centers are needed? The rich and powerful only see profits, while the rest of us watch our beautiful landscape disappear." Higgins pulled a handkerchief from his pocket and wiped his forehead. It was late afternoon, but the sun, even under the shade tree, was still blazing hot.

"Nicely put. I'll include it in the article. Thank you for your time, Mr. Higgins. I wish you luck on selling your farm, and I'm sorry it's come to this."

Higgins pushed his hands into his pockets. "Me too. I feel like I've let my ancestors down. My grandpa would be sorely disappointed."

"Don't forget, he had this place when small family farms were still profitable. You can't blame yourself for the way things worked out."

"Thanks. You're right." He took a deep breath. "I'm going to look toward my future now. Time with the grandchildren, that's my next adventure in life."

I was pleased that he had somewhere to go, another purpose to pursue, but as much as he tried to put on a brave face about it, having to sell his family's farm had dropped a heavy weight on his shoulders. Rupert Madison deserved a kick in the pants.

CHAPTER 10

*L*ana invited me for a summer salad dinner, but it came with a price. She'd gotten behind with her work and desperately needed my help filling the treat bags for movie night. I always looked forward to spending time with my sisters, but it was hard when I had something heavy on my mind, something I couldn't discuss with them. I hadn't heard from Jackson all day, and the silence had left me feeling even more bereft. I decided to slap on a brave face and help Lana with her task. It would be a nice diversion from my negative thoughts. I hadn't had any time to formulate my talk with Edward. I wasn't even convinced it would be a good idea. Then, I'd be stuck with a moody ghost on top of a moody boyfriend.

Lana had prepared a delicious spinach and strawberry salad. We ate out on her back patio and finished the meal with iced coffees topped with whipped cream. We talked about nothing in particular. Lana was one of those people who liked to dominate the conversation. I was more than happy to let her go on about her latest client, a bride whose mother-in-law was so stereotypical, Lana shuddered a few times while talking about the woman.

The mother-in-law was paying for half the wedding, so she'd decided that meant she got to make a hundred percent of the decisions. She contradicted everything the bride suggested and changed everything from the flowers to the cake flavors. I told her it would serve the woman right if the bride and groom just snuck off to elope. She agreed.

The humidity outside urged us back into the coolness of the house. The chocolates for the treat bags wouldn't survive the heat either. What I hadn't factored in about the pleasant, diverting evening was that I'd be stuck staring at Rupert Madison's big face as I filled the bags. The candy bars with his picture on the wrappers were more comical than the cardboard cutouts, and that was saying a lot.

"I've never known a man more in love with his own likeness," I said as I pushed a bar into a cellophane bag. The bags were printed with tiny gold stars. We tied each one off with a strand of bright blue curling ribbon. Sample sizes of red licorice, sour gummies, chocolate covered raisins and pretzels rounded out the treat bags.

"It's true, Rupert Madison is fond of himself. A few years back, I planned an event for the opening of one of his communities." She said the last word with enough of a sour lemon twist that I knew she felt the same way about his characterless houses and neighborhoods. "He had a massive banner printed with his face on it. It was almost frightening, a six-foot-tall head staring down at everyone as they ate their burgers and hot dogs."

"I had a terrible run-in with the man today." I tied off a ribbon and dragged a scissor along it to give it its signature curl. "He fired a worker just for tossing an apple core on the ground. It happened to roll under Madison's foot right after I'd enraged him by bringing up the poor quality of his homes." I sat back with a gasp. "My gosh, it was my fault. I might have gotten that poor man fired. Madison was angry at me, and the timing—well—

now I feel bad. The poor guy was so distraught. I spoke up to Madison afterward and let him know, in no uncertain terms, what I thought of him."

Lana laughed. "I would have loved to see that. I couldn't wait for his contract with me to be over. I couldn't stand the man. His father, Henry Madison, was always a well-respected businessman and developer. He was honest and had integrity. His son—not so much."

"Apples sometimes *do* fall far from the tree, it seems." I finished another bag and set it in one of the boxes Lana had set up for collecting the treats.

Lana's curling technique was far more skilled than mine. As she pulled the scissor blade along the ribbon, it rolled up into perfect Shirley Temple ringlets. "So, are you going to tell me what's wrong?" she asked casually and without looking up from her task.

"I told you I had an unpleasant run-in with Madison." My sister didn't have a sixth sense. She didn't even believe that Raine had it, but she sure knew when I was feeling off-balance. I'd been convinced I was doing a stellar job of hiding it. I supposed some things were just too hard to hide behind a forced smile.

"Not talking about Madison." Lana finally looked up. "Something is bothering you. You're wearing it all out on your sleeve, only you have that sleeve rolled up in an attempt to hide it from your very astute sister."

"It's nothing. Besides, I already talked about it with Raine." I knew that confession was a mistake the second it left my mouth.

Lana stared at me, not saying a word.

"I know, I know, but sometimes, when I'm having problems, it's nice to talk to someone outside my sister circle." Of course, the real reason I spoke to Raine first and only could never be revealed. "You have your friend from college, Georgie. I know you talk to her whenever you feel like hearing advice from someone other than a sister." I should have been a lawyer. My argument sufficed.

"Fine. I suppose you should have secrets from Emily and me."

"No secrets. (Only a massive one that would explain everything and, at the same time, freak my sisters out.) I just need to work something out. Raine gave me some tips on how to deal with it."

"All right. Understood." It was obvious she didn't, but I wasn't going to argue. She ripped open a package of licorice with more force than needed and handed me a red strand. "Here. Remember Mom used to buy those big tubs of red licorice, and we'd spend all summer with them hanging from our mouths?"

"Then Emily threw up red and mom blamed us. As if we were force feeding her the candy."

"That's because as far as Mom was concerned her little angel-on-earth never did anything wrong. Boy, that was disgusting. You know, I don't think Emily's eaten a piece of licorice since."

"Can you blame her?" We both laughed. I was more than relieved to have the subject changed. Lana knew that too. That was why she opened the licorice. Even though I didn't want to talk to Lana about this unique problem, it was always comforting to know I had a big sister so in tune with my feelings she knew when something wasn't right. And this week felt anything but right.

CHAPTER 11

*I*t had been an exhausting day. Even so, I hadn't gotten much accomplished other than irritating Rupert Madison and helping Lana fill treat bags. As tired as I was, I knew if I dropped into bed too early, I'd stare at the ceiling for a long time. Jackson had basically ghosted me all day. On top of that, my literal ghost was following me around the house like a stray puppy. He knew something was amiss. Normally, he'd ask me straight out what was wrong, but he had incredible intuition for someone who existed only in spirit. He knew not to approach the problem because it had something to do with him.

It wasn't as if Edward Beckett had asked to be trapped in the Cider Ridge Inn for eternity. I was sure, if given the chance, he'd move on. But since all my attempts to make that happen had failed, he was here to stay. At least for the foreseeable future. Now, I worried that future would not include Jackson.

I sat at the table with a glass of milk. I hoped it would help lull me into a sleepy coma. Redford and Newman had gone off to bed without me, so I had the kitchen to myself. With one notable exception.

It was hard to fathom how one incorporeal being could show so much emotion on his face. "You're not off to bed yet?" he asked quietly.

I lifted the glass of milk. "Having a nightcap first. Hoping it'll help me sleep."

His blue gaze scrutinized my face. "You look tired."

"Yep. I'm feeling tired too. Just need something to take the edge off."

"Edge of what?" he asked.

I shook my head. "Not in the mood for a twentieth century phrase lesson tonight." I was also absolutely not in the mood to bring up the weighty issue I needed to discuss with Edward. That was going to take far more energy and nerve than I had at the moment.

Edward drifted to the window and stared out into the night. There was just enough moonlight to give the front yard a glow.

"What are you thinking about, Edward?" I asked.

"I was thinking about that day—" He continued to stare out the window. "My last day. We held the duel right out there, in the field. Cleveland was so angry, he could hardly speak. I thought he might die from rage even before shots were fired."

I sat forward with interest. Cleveland was the man who bested Edward in the duel that ended his life. "I've always meant to ask you—how come you were not a better shot? I would expect a man like you, with your privileged upbringing, and especially at that time in history, to have been very skilled with a gun. But you clearly lost that duel."

"If I'd allowed myself, I could have shot off every button on Cleveland's waistcoat before he fired his gun." He stated it as fact with none of the usual posh arrogance that went with his bragging.

"I don't understand," I said.

Edward floated over toward the table. He gazed down at me

for a long moment, not speaking. It was his way of apologizing. He knew. He knew he was the cause of my current turmoil, and he seemed to understand that I wasn't ready to talk about it. I always found his past, when he was mortal, intriguing. I needed something to take my mind off my woes.

Edward pulled his gaze away and drifted back toward the window. This time he didn't stare out. He looked at me. "I tried to talk the fool out of it. I'd grown up hunting and shooting. I always had a natural talent for it. My father hated that I was better than him. In my teens, I was so much better than him and most of the men he kept company with that he stopped allowing me to ride along with the hunting parties. Every boy and man in the county would head out for a weekend hunt, but I was left behind. He would blame it on my behavior or some meaningless mishap. I was being punished merely because he didn't want to look inferior to me."

"So, instead of being filled with pride that his son was such a skilled marksman, he was ashamed. Ashamed because he couldn't compete."

"Exactly."

"Every story I hear about your family gives me a worse opinion of them. You were cast off as the black sheep, but it seemed they were the cause of your rebellion."

"Sometimes it was hard to know who to despise more, my controlling, vain mother or my cruel, selfish father."

"Sounded as if they were competing for the worst parent title. That still doesn't explain what happened in the duel. Maybe Cleveland was more skilled than you realized."

"Impossible. I'd been on several hunts with the man. He couldn't hit a deer if it walked right up to him and rested its head in his lap."

"Then why on earth would he challenge you to a duel, and how did it end so badly for you?"

"I'd shamed him. Back then, the only way to save your pride and your reputation was to challenge the offender to a duel."

"I'm certainly glad that barbaric tradition was eventually outlawed."

Edward smiled. "Seems like these days they go straight to the cowardly way and shoot someone dead. No duel. No challenge with rules and seconds to keep things civil. Straight to murder."

I nodded. "You're right. Maybe an official challenge to a duel was less barbaric. You said it had to do with being slighted, with hurt pride. I don't know where it would stop. I could see someone challenging their neighbor to a duel for allowing their sprinkler to hit their car. It seems like people are always angry or feeling slighted about something."

Edward looked at me sympathetically. "Was it something I said or did?" he asked. The subject had changed, but I wasn't ready to get deep into it.

"It's something the three of us need to talk about, but not now."

Edward knew exactly which three I was talking about.

"Forgive me," he said. "I'll try harder. I don't like seeing you in distress."

"I don't like feeling it. Back to the duel. What happened? Why did you lose if you were clearly more skilled with a pistol?"

Edward shook his head, slowly enough that all his features stayed in placed. Occasionally, he would move too fast, and it would take a few seconds for everything to catch up and fall back into place. That was what Jackson had teased him about the night of the barn dinner. It was one of the crueler things I'd heard Jackson say to Edward. That was when I knew the situation had gone from bad to worse.

"Bonnie, his wife, was hysterical. She begged Cleveland to reconsider. She pleaded with me too. I told her I'd gladly forfeit and walk away from everything. I had no place to go, but I'd obviously overstayed my welcome."

"You were having an affair with Cleveland's wife," I reminded him unnecessarily. "The first clandestine kiss was your clue that you'd overstayed. Fathering a child was an even bigger clue."

"Yes, well, as you noted earlier, my family did not instill the best decision-making skills or the finest sense of moral character. I was hurt. Kat, the woman I loved, had left to marry her betrothed. My family had disinherited me. I was stripped of fortune, title and, frankly, any will to go on with life."

His last sentence made me sit up from my tired slump. "Edward, you didn't—did you? Did you let Cleveland shoot you?"

Edward turned back to the window. "Not exactly. Bonnie was standing on the front steps. Her maid was holding her back, keeping her from running down the steps to interfere with the duel. She was screaming and crying, telling Cleveland not to go through with it. I couldn't leave her without a husband. I had no idea she was carrying my child at the time. I only knew that it was time for me to leave for good. Cleveland wasn't going to be satisfied unless he was allowed to take at least one shot at me. He was not skilled with a hunting rifle, and I assumed it would be the same with a pistol. I thought I might get away with a small, superficial wound. Something insignificant enough to allow me to ride away."

I winced. "Was he better with a pistol?"

"Good lord, no. He was an absolute imbecile with a weapon. Just as the count ended, and we turned to face each other, Bonnie sprang free from her maid's grasp and ran toward us. Both of us looked her direction. As Cleveland turned to tell his wife to go back, his pistol went off. The bullet found its target. It wasn't the grazing flesh wound I'd hoped for. I knew instantly that it would take my life. Bonnie insisted on having the servants carry me inside. I begged her to let me die on the grass under the clear blue sky. She wouldn't hear of it. She was certain I would survive."

The duel had always been a subject we tiptoed around. Hearing the whole thing narrated from start to finish was nothing short of stunning.

"Bonnie caused it," I said. "She must have been heartbroken."

"I don't think that was how she saw it. Cleveland fired the bullet. She swore to me as I lay dying that she would never forgive him for it. That was when she informed me that she was with child and that I was the father."

"A very dramatic ending to a chaos-filled life, Lord Beckett." I never referred to him by title. It seemed appropriate in the moment, but Edward didn't agree.

"I was never Lord Beckett. My title was stripped far before my father's death. He took it with him to the grave until one of my sniveling, unworthy cousins took over."

"I know. It's just you died in such a wild, almost romantic way, it felt right saying it. You gave up your life because you didn't want Bonnie to be without her husband."

"A lot of good that did. He sent her off as soon as he discovered she was with child." This time he whipped around toward me with enough motion to send his image into a small tornado before settling in one spot. "Why don't you send him a message on your small metal box, like you always do?"

"Who? Oh, you mean Jackson." I stared at my phone sitting next to my glass of milk. "Not tonight. Sometimes time and silence are what's needed."

"I see. Will you be all right?" he asked.

"Of course, I will. I'm off to bed. I think I'll be out the second my head hits the pillow. Goodnight, Edward."

"Goodnight, Sunni."

CHAPTER 12

I arrived at the newsroom. I needed to get out of the house to get some work done. Normally, I enjoyed working at my kitchen table, but I couldn't concentrate at home. Everything reminded me of Jackson. The kitchen cabinet he'd fixed last week, the snacks in the pantry that were mostly his choice, even my adorable goats Sassy and Coco only received a few hugs because they reminded me too much of the heartache I was feeling.

I reached for the newsroom door, opened it and poked my head inside. Myrna spotted my surreptitious survey of the room.

"It's all right. She's out buying some new drapes for her office," Myrna said with a laugh. "You're safe, and I want to hear all about it."

I stepped inside. Parker was hiding a grin behind his monitor. "I hear you gave ole Rupert a tongue lashing," he said. "Wish I'd been there," he added.

"You're not the only one. I should have taped it. The whole incident only lasted seconds, but I'm sure it would have gone viral." I placed my things on my desk and leaned against the front of it. "Do I still have a job?" I asked.

"Far as I know," Parker said. "Prue didn't seem too mad about it. Rupert called her personally."

I flinched. "So, he made good on his threat."

Parker leaned back on his chair. It squeaked and rolled back. "He'll come crawling back. There aren't any other papers in the area that have as high a circulation—"

"And that's because of Sunni Taylor's column," Myrna interjected with a smile.

"That's sweet of you, Myrna."

"It's true," Parker said. It was rare for him to be so flattering. Boy, did I need it. I drove the whole distance to town thinking I'd walk into an ambush and a pink slip. It would have been the appropriate ending to a terrible few days.

"Thank you, guys. I needed to hear that. Do you really think I still have a job?" I asked.

"Of course," Myrna said. "I think Prue's exact words after Madison's phone call were 'I'll be happy not to have to see his smug face in my newspaper anymore.'"

Parker tapped a pile of folders on his desk. "We've got a waiting list for advertisement space. I've been making calls all morning. People are excited to finally get a placement in the paper."

"That's such a relief." The newsroom door opened as I sat down. My heart raced ahead. My two colleagues had assured me that Prudence was not upset about losing the Madison account, but I wouldn't be truly relieved until I heard it straight from her.

I relaxed when Myrna's friend, Joanne, walked through the door. I had a few more minutes of reprieve before Prudence returned. Joanne was a member of the dance troupe Myrna belonged to. She was carrying a garment on a hanger. It was covered by a gray bag. "Here's your costume, Myrna. I finished the alterations this morning. That skirt should fit better now."

Myrna blushed pink. "I blame it on all those pastries Prudence brings to work. Thank you for doing this, Joanne, and if we could keep those alterations between you and me." She handed Joanne a twenty-dollar bill. Joanne tucked the bill discreetly into her pocket. It was all done with a clandestine tone and glance. I felt as if I was watching an illegal drug transaction instead of a friend with sewing talent handing off an altered dance costume. It wasn't the first time Myrna'd had problems with a costume. She was probably right in blaming the pastries. As Myrna once pointed out, I ate one and then left the office, but she was stuck there all day, breathing in their sugary goodness.

"See you at ten," Joanne said and headed out.

"That's right. Your dance group is performing at the fair," I said. "How fun."

"I'm so nervous about it. I'm in the front row." Myrna unzipped the garment bag and checked out the costume before zipping it back up. It seemed to be mostly pink lace.

"I'm sure you'll be great." I opened my laptop and pulled out my notepad. The front door opened again. This time it was Prudence. I hadn't had time to panic.

"Sunni, you're here. I'd like to see you in my office." She marched purposefully past and headed straight to her office.

I looked at my two coworkers. Parker returned a shrug, and Myrna bit her lip with worry. Not exactly the pep talk I was hoping for.

I grabbed my notebook and grimaced as I walked past Myrna's desk. Prudence had left her office door ajar, but I knocked. It seemed like the right choice given the situation.

"Come in, Sunni. I was expecting you. That is why I left the door open." She said it as if I was being ridiculous, but I was sure if I hadn't knocked first, she would have lectured me on waiting to be invited inside rather than barging in.

Prudence's office was always filled with a perfume-laden cloud of plug-in air freshener. Today's fragrance smelled like an artificial flower garden. I pressed my hand against my nose to stifle a sneeze.

"Have a seat, please."

I sat in the plush, upholstered chair she'd had made especially for office guests. The cushions released a perfumed puff of air, a collection of all the scents she'd plugged in for the last six months mingled together in one overwhelming fragrance. I pressed my nose again.

Prudence yanked a tissue from her tissue box. The box was enrobed in a lavender crocheted cover, like a tea cozy, except for tissue boxes.

I took the tissue and wiped my nose.

"I hope you're not getting a cold," she said while shuffling a few papers around her desk.

"No, I'm fine. What did you need to see me about?" I decided it was best to get right to it. If she was going to fire me, I'd rather get it over with. Then, I could go home, pull a carton of ice cream out of my freezer and sit in bed for the rest of the day.

"I'm sure you've heard—" She looked pointedly toward the newsroom. "Mr. Rupert Madison has pulled his advertising budget from the paper."

"I can explain why I was so terse with him."

"No need. Madison is a bully and a cheat and a disgrace to his good father's name. His wife, Monica, was a friend of mine. We belonged to the same social circle. She got wise about five years ago. Packed up the kids and moved to Hawaii, of all places."

"Hawaii? Nice choice."

Prudence's nose crinkled. "If you like all that sand and sun, I suppose. The point is—you probably did the paper a favor by scaring him off."

I sat up straighter. "My pleasure."

"That said—" Her tone turned harsher and her expression grew sterner. "In the future, please refrain from speaking your mind so freely. You're out there to get information for articles, not to make enemies for the paper."

I shrank back down. I almost would rather have been fired than scolded like a child. It wasn't what I needed right then.

"Understood. Anything else?" I asked curtly.

"That'll be all."

I got up and walked out. The newsroom had seemed like a good idea this morning. I was regretting that decision.

CHAPTER 13

My irritation and general state of mood helped me pound out a fast and furious article on my keyboard. Once I got started, I didn't stop. Myrna laughed at one point and told me to "come up for air." A good reporter never blurred the line between a news piece and an opinion piece, but I broke that rule. I started out letting the readers know that Rupert Madison would be building a large shopping center off Kent Road and that a local farmer would be forced to sell a piece of land that had been handed down through generations because the noise and chaos of a large building project and eventual shopping center would make it impossible to keep farming his land. I also made a list of all the shopping centers within a ten-mile radius that had vacant buildings because stores had shut down. People shopped online now. The traditional way of driving to a store to, possibly, find the thing you were looking for had been replaced by the convenience of finding anything you wanted, no matter how unusual or rare, and then having that sought-after item delivered to your door. It wasn't only opinion.

What I said about the undeniable ease of shopping online was fact. The empty buildings were fact too.

I might have been buttering my already burnt toast with the somewhat lopsided article, but I finished it and sent it off to Prudence for her approval. I then made a quick, cowardly exit from the newsroom. I didn't want to miss Myrna's performance.

The end-of-summer fair was in full swing. A mix of *fair* aromas — grilled burgers, cotton candy and fruity snow cones — rolled out over the entire park. Outshining the Rupert Madison cutouts in every possible way was a large vintage movie poster of *Butch Cassidy and the Sundance Kid* displayed at the entrance. Something told me the real Butch and Sundance didn't have chiseled jaws, lake blue eyes and pearly white smiles. Redford and Newman were certainly a pair—both the actors and the dogs. While the real Sundance probably didn't look like Redford, he was known as a lightning-fast gunslinger. I'd fallen asleep quickly the night before and hadn't given Edward's whole story much thought until this morning. There were so many more layers to the man than I first thought. Yes, he had arrogance and being pompous down to an art, but the more I learned about his history, the more I realized he had a good heart and soul.

"Sunni!" Lauren strolled toward me on white sandals. She was still wearing the visor with the enormous bill. "Are you here to see Myrna? They're warming up behind the stage." A portable stage had been set up at one corner of the park. Aside from the dance troupe, the local high schools were set to show off their orchestras and choral groups. It was usually hot and sticky enough that at least one choral singer passed out from standing too long in the sun. Today, the temperature was less brutal than it had been over the weekend, but the humidity hung around like a wet blanket.

"Hey, Lauren!" a group of young people called as they headed across the grass toward the stage.

"Hey, guys!" Covering the fair was the perfect assignment for Lauren. She knew everyone, and most of the attendees were young. It was an event to mark the end of a long summer and remind kids that school days were around the corner. It was a bittersweet celebration for the young people in town.

Lauren wrapped her arm around mine. "I heard you gave it good to that greedy man, Rupert Madison. The thing is—hardly anyone cares about a new shopping center. I think he's going to regret building it. It's going to cost a lot of money, but the revenue isn't going to be flowing in like he thinks. He'll lose a lot of money."

"Unfortunately, when extremely rich people lose money, they easily recoup it by claiming a tax loss. I suppose that's why he's willing to take the financial risk. But I agree. A shopping center seems antiquated."

Lauren held tightly to my arm. She seemed to be directing me toward the game booths. I had my heart set more on the food kiosks. "I thought you might want to try the dunk tank. Only the line is very long." Lauren tugged my arm. We stopped a good twenty yards from the dunk tank. The reflection off the Plexiglass front of the booth made it hard to see who was sitting inside of it.

I lifted my sunglasses to get a better look. "Is that—?"

"Sure is. Rupert Madison. No one's dunked him yet, but the man standing at the front of the line has spent about twenty bucks trying to do it."

I moved so I could see the front of the line. The young man running the booth was handing a softball to none other than Robert Higgins. He had a look of angry determination on his face as he pulled his arm back and let the ball fly. The ball missed the paddle by a good foot.

"Wish that line wasn't so long," I said. "I could take him down with the first shot."

"Lauren leaned away and peered at me from under her giant

visor bill. "No kidding? Myrna told me you used to play sports in high school."

"I was a pitcher." I rolled my shoulder. "A pretty darn good one at that, but I'm a little out of practice."

"Come on, give someone else a chance," a voice called from back in the line.

Rupert sat fully clothed in a t-shirt and shorts. I was sure he wasn't used to being so casually dressed in public. He seemed more of an expensively-tailored-suit kind of guy, but he made this exception, possibly to show everyone he was one of the regular folks. He had taken the opportunity to advertise his future shopping center by having a picture of it ironed onto the front of the shirt. Higgins had to face down both his enemy and the shopping mall that would eventually surround his family farm. For that reason, he was reluctant to give up his place in the line.

The young man running the game finally insisted that the next person in line be given a chance. Rupert grinned behind the Plexiglass as Higgins shoved his money back into his pocket and got out of line. A young boy stepped forward, flanked by his father. The dad crouched down and explained where the ball needed to land to dunk the man in the booth.

A nice looking, twenty-something man with several tattoos and a bright green tank shirt came up to us. "Lauren, how's it going?"

"Mikey, hey, how are you?" Lauren smiled my direction. "Mikey and I went to high school together. This is my mentor and coworker at the *Junction Times*, Sunni Taylor."

Mikey had a great smile. He stuck out his hand. A skull and crossbones was tattooed on the back of it. "Sunni Taylor," he repeated as I shook his hand. "My mom likes your articles. Can I get a selfie with you? My mom would love it."

"Sure." I leaned in and he lifted his phone for a selfie.

"Cool, thanks."

"Mikey, is that Jeremy Sexton in line?" Lauren asked.

It took me a second to remember where I'd heard the name before. Seeing the tall, thin man with his stringy, dark hair and loose-fitting clothing helped. It was the worker Madison fired so abruptly because of a misplaced apple core. He was next in line behind the little boy. The child was begging his dad to pay for one more try.

"Yep, that's him." Mikey crossed his arms in front of him. "This should be good. Jeremy was a pitcher on our high school team," he explained to me. "Jeremy is one of those guys who's good at everything… except keeping a job," he added.

"Oh?" Lauren asked. "I thought he was working for Madison on home building. Not many people would be brave enough to dunk their own boss."

"Jeremy isn't working for Madison anymore," I said before Mikey could bring it up. They both looked at me in question.

"I was at the worksite yesterday interviewing Madison. Jeremy tossed aside an apple core. It happened to land right in Madison's path."

Lauren's chin dropped. "Do you mean that he was fired for throwing an apple core?"

"Unfortunately," I said. "I feel like it was my fault. I'd angered Madison by grilling him about the quality of his homes."

"Just a step above a gingerbread house, according to my dad," Mikey said. "He's an architect."

"Madison definitely didn't want to hear about his shabbily built houses," I said.

"Wait, here we go." Mikey waved his arm toward the tank. Jeremy handed off his dollar.

Rupert sat up straighter. His smug grin vanished, and he gripped the edges of the platform.

"Looks like someone isn't looking too confident anymore," Lauren noted.

Jeremy wound up like a true pitcher. He lifted his leg, pulled his arm back and let it rip. The softball landed right in the center of the paddle. A bell rang and the platform gave way dumping Rupert Madison into the water. Loud cheers and applause followed.

Lauren laughed. "Madison sure doesn't have a fan club around here. Remember that nail Deborah pulled from one of the cardboard cutouts? Since then, three more of Madison's paper doll likenesses have been vandalized. Someone even punched his face so hard the cardboard neck broke in half. His head dangled back and forth in the breeze."

"Nothing to like about the man," Mikey said. "Jeremy said he was a terrible man to work for. I guess I'll go congratulate him. Sweet slice of revenge. He needed it. Nice meeting you."

"You as well."

It took several event staff people to help Madison out of the tank. He dripped water and looked extremely grumpy as someone put a beach towel around his shoulders.

"So much for trying to be one of the gang," I said.

Lauren laughed. "He looks as if he's regretting his decision to join in the fun."

I smiled at her. "I don't know who enjoyed that more, Jeremy or me."

CHAPTER 14

After a long morning at the fair, eating unhealthy amounts of artificial coloring, sugar and whatever else went into the delicious but highly processed fair foods, I headed home to rest. Prudence sent an email that she'd received my story. None of her usual comments followed. I had no idea what her silence meant, but I had other things to think about. Namely, that I had two tickets to movie night, but Jackson hadn't texted or called. I toyed with the idea of calling him first, then I reminded myself that he'd been the one to walk away angry. The next move was his.

A long, cool shower refreshed me enough that I decided to get dressed and go to the movie without my date. Edward was still keeping a low profile, and that was fine with me.

A nearly full moon wasn't ideal for movie night under the stars, and a slight breeze had kicked up to make the screen wobble and shudder. That hadn't stopped people from attending. Movie night was always a popular social event. The movies they played were old classics, ones most attendees had seen many times. It was more about the nostalgia of sitting under the stars and watching a familiar classic with people they knew, people who lived in the same community.

A long line of moviegoers stood at the popcorn cart. An equally long line had formed with people anxious to get their treat bags. What was a movie without red licorice and a Rupert Madison candy bar?

Madison was standing with a small cluster of people gathered at a group of chairs on the far side of the seating area. I couldn't help but notice that Veronica Blaine was standing with her own group just across the way. Dirty looks and scowls seemed to be shooting both directions. So much for nostalgia and community togetherness.

The folding chairs had been arranged in casual rows and clusters in front of the fifteen-foot-high movie screen. A rolling cart topped with a projector and laptop sat in the center of the chairs waiting to splash Paul Newman and Robert Redford across the screen.

A small dais and microphone had been set up to the right of the stage. Deborah, the woman in charge of the event, was testing the microphone with a few taps and the obligatory "testing, one, two, three." She looked sunburned and frazzled from the long day.

My phone vibrated in my pocket. I pulled it out expecting to see Lana or Emily's name. It was Jackson. My heart thumped a few times before I ran my thumb across the screen to open the text. "Got called out to Hickory Flats for a possible homicide. Won't make the movie." That was the entire message. I didn't know what to make of it. The obvious part was that he was working, and he wouldn't be here for movie night. That was not too surprising. But the text came through as if we'd been talking on and off all day, and this was a casual courtesy message telling me not to wait for him at the movie. I

MOVIE NIGHT MADNESS

grunted in frustration and pushed the phone back into my pocket.

Deborah had a microphone, but she had to speak loudly to get everyone's attention. "Excuse me, please, quiet down. Please, everyone, quiet down." It took a few minutes, not surprisingly, but lively conversations slowed to a murmur and then to silence.

Once she concluded she had everyone's attention, Deborah cleared her throat and leaned closer to the microphone. "Welcome to Firefly's annual end-of-summer fair and movie night under the stars."

Everyone clapped and cheered. Deborah had fretted when I spoke up about everything going well. It seemed I hadn't cursed the event after all. It had been a pleasant, fun-filled day with no unfortunate incidents. I considered Rupert's dunking the highlight of the whole affair. He might have disagreed.

"We'll be starting our movie shortly. I'd like to thank Betty Ingrid and Arlene Bustos for picking tonight's feature *Butch Cassidy and the Sundance Kid*."

"Figures two women were behind the choice," Lana said from behind.

I spun around. "I thought you weren't coming."

Lana held up a ticket. "Deborah told me I earned a free ticket because I put together the treat bags, and since it's, you know, Redford and Newman, I thought I could pull on some decent shorts and shoes and make an appearance." Lana glanced around. "Where's your personal Redford?"

"You mean my dog? I don't think he'd like this many people."

Lana rolled her eyes. "I was talking about that tall, hunky-as-a-movie-star guy you're occasionally known to be seen with."

"He got called to Hickory Flats for a possible homicide." I was lucky I had a ready-to-go excuse. If I'd hesitated for even a second, Lana would have spent the entire movie grilling me about it.

"What a shame," Lana said. "Oh, here we go. Mr. Big has to put in his two cents and let everyone know he basically funded the whole shebang."

Rupert Madison was wearing gray slacks, a blue Polo shirt and brown loafers, his idea of movie night casual, as he made his way up to the microphone.

"Good evening, Firefly Junction," he boomed into the microphone. It squealed in response. He tapped it to stop the horrid noise. "I'm glad everyone made it to this wonderful event. Madison Homes is a proud sponsor of the end-of-summer fair. I think Deborah Jones deserves a round of applause for making it such a success." A round of applause echoed across the park. Rupert waited for the noise to stop before continuing. "I have some great news for our community. My company will be teaming with Eggers Construction to break ground on the new Madison Shopping Center a month from today." The announcement was made with great enthusiasm, but the audience didn't return the same amount of zeal. It was the opposite, in fact. There were a number of people booing him, and it wasn't only coming from Veronica's group.

Rupert's grin sank. He looked angered and flustered. "I know some of you have already formed a negative opinion of the project due to propaganda being pushed out by a handful of people." He looked pointedly at Veronica.

She lifted her chin in response. "It's not propaganda. No one wants your vanity project. This is all about you and your greed and your power."

Deborah stepped in. Her fair had gone off without a hitch, and she wasn't about to let a feud start before the movie. She took charge of the microphone. "I think most of us are here to see a movie, so let's find our seats. And please, try and keep your wrappers and drink cups together. It's a little breezy tonight, and the cleanup crew already has their work cut out for them. Without further ado, let's start the movie." She switched off the microphone before speaking to Rupert with an apologetic smile.

"Guess the pre-movie entertainment is over," Lana remarked.

"Sure seems that way."

CHAPTER 15

My sister, Lana, made a cowardly early exit twenty minutes before the movie ended. She claimed it was because she disliked the end scene where the Bolivian police take Butch and Sundance out in a proverbial "blaze of glory." It was a scene the directors had really dragged out. Since there was always some question about the true end for the two infamous outlaws, Lana preferred to think of them as still alive, riding around the South American desert with their cool hats and Hollywood smiles. When it came to Lana's real motive, I knew better. Lana had an extremely popular business, one that was based on her *fame* in the community as the go-to party planner for weddings, anniversaries and company soirees. Her success was based far more on the amazing results she produced than on her social ties. She kept mostly to herself when it came to her personal life, and she liked it that way.

Speakers had been set up around the seating area to give the audience the fully immersive experience of a raging gunfight. As the famous freeze frame of Butch and Sundance running toward their inevitable death rolled up, the audience applauded. Lively

MOVIE NIGHT MADNESS

conversations started back up. The end of the movie heralded in the official end of summer. A picturesque fall was just around the corner.

Deborah hurried to her microphone to shout out a few last words before everyone dispersed. She had to yell loudly to get attention. Most people were already out of their seats and ready to leave.

"Please, pick up your area. Large trash cans have been placed around the seating area. Find one and throw away your trash. The cleanup crew is tired, and they'd like to go home too." She continued, speaking as fast and loud as she could. Like Lana always said, '*Some people grab onto a microphone, and they never let go.*' "Thank you for attending the Firefly Junction end-of-summer movie night." People were hurrying to beat the traffic jam out of the parking lot, but that didn't stop Deborah. "We collected a great deal of money for that new fountain in front of city hall. It was a very successful day." There was some mild applause in various locations around the park. "Good night, every—"

A scream interrupted her farewell. A second scream followed. It came from the far side of the seating area. I shoved the trash I'd been holding into my popcorn bag, then raced between the seats to where a group of people stood around looking positively horrified.

"Someone call an ambulance," a person yelled from somewhere within the stunned crowd.

I elbowed my way to the center of attention. Rupert Madison was leaning back in his chair, eyes closed and his arms hanging limply at his sides. If not for the blood dripping from the back of his head, it would have been easy to conclude he was sleeping. But he wasn't sleeping. By all appearances, Rupert Madison was dead.

"Let me through. I'm a doctor," someone said behind me.

"Let Dr. Turnbill through," someone else said.

I stepped aside as Dr. Turnbill pushed to the center of the circle. His heavy brows hopped up high on his forehead as he got a good look at Rupert. "Oh my," he muttered quietly enough that only I heard him. A frantic energy buzzed around the onlookers.

"Is he dead?" I heard people asking in hushed tones.

"It looks as if someone shot him," another clearer voice said. People gasped in response.

"Call the police," someone else suggested.

I stretched up and looked over the worried faces. Park lights had been shut down for the movie. They popped back on suddenly, lighting up each corner of the park with a bright glow. Standing a good distance away from the center of attention was Veronica Blaine and her small entourage. They looked as horrified as everyone else. Veronica had her arms crossed, and she was nervously looking around. I tucked that reaction away for later.

Dr. Turnbill picked up Madison's limp hand. He was a doctor. He knew before he even went through the show of searching for a pulse that he wouldn't find one. His expressive brows relaxed.

"What is it, Dr. Turnbill? Shouldn't you do something?" someone asked.

Turnbill's face dropped.. "I'm sorry. Rupert Madison is dead."

A louder gasp and more frantic discussion followed. Sirens screeched on the road leading to the park. "We should give the officials room to get through," I said.

Turnbill nodded. "Yes, she's right. Everyone, there's nothing more to see here. Please step back."

Something I'd always observed at a murder scene—some people were more than eager to leave the area. Others stuck around to satisfy that morbid spark of curiosity we all had. It was the inner urge that made us slow down to look at an accident. About half the crowd dispersed eagerly. If someone had shot Rupert Madison, it stood to reason that there was an armed killer somewhere in the park. My instinct would be to head home quickly, but my investigative instinct told me I'd just stumbled onto another murder case. While most people were milling about in dazed confusion muttering phrases like "who would do such a thing" and "are we all in danger," the big question on my mind was "which detective would they call to the crime scene?" Was I prepared to come face-to-face with Detective Jackson? Not really. Not tonight.

A patrol car rolled in ahead of the ambulance. I was relieved that Dr. Turnbill was there to fill the officers and paramedics in on the situation. I stepped back from the area to take a look around and discovered my coworker sitting on a bench, hugging herself. Lauren looked pale and scared. She was so sure of herself, so incredible and worldly, I tended to forget that she was still very young and innocent.

I sat on the bench next to her. "I guess this is your first dead body," I said.

She took a deep breath and released the tight grip she had on herself. "I know we journalists are supposed to be tougher and all that…"

"Nonsense." I put my arm around her shoulder. "A dead body is shocking no matter who you are. Dr. Turnbill turned so pale, I thought he might pass out." It was a slight exaggeration, but she didn't need to know that.

Lauren looked at me. "But you don't seem to mind it."

"That's because I'm a freak."

A laugh spurted from her mouth. She quickly covered it. "Oh my gosh, I can't believe I laughed when there's a dead man right over there."

I squeezed her shoulders. "That's all right. I don't think he heard you."

She elbowed me lightly. "Stop. You'll make me laugh again. How come you're not bothered by it?"

"I'm bothered by it plenty. But murder scenes intrigue me. I immediately want to know who snapped. Who got angry enough with the victim that they decided murder was the only way out?"

"I guess you've found exactly the right soulmate in Jax since he's a homicide detective."

I nodded, unable to agree verbally. Was he my soulmate? It sure seemed that way these past few years.

"Detective Jackson is going to have his work cut out with this one," Lauren continued. "Rupert Madison was not a popular man. How did he die?"

I hadn't taken the time yet to analyze what had happened. "I think someone shot him."

Lauren sucked in a sharp breath. "In the middle of all these people? And no one noticed? How on earth did they pull it off?"

"Those are all great questions." I smiled at her. "You're becoming quite the reporter."

She smiled back. "That means a lot."

It had been a long, hot day, but Lauren was on assignment. She'd stuck it out the entire day to get the story, a story that now had a shocking, tragic ending. Had I jinxed Deborah's smooth-running event, after all? I was sure she hadn't expected such a terrible ending to an otherwise great day.

"How come Jax wasn't with you tonight?" The conversation had been going along so smoothly, darn it.

"He was planning on it, but he got called away to Hickory Flats for a possible homicide."

"I suppose you're used to that. Jax cancelling plans at the last minute. I admire you. I don't know if I could partner with someone who was always on call."

My throat was tightening as she spoke. "Yeah, it's hard," was all I could get out.

She grabbed my hand. "I've upset you. I don't know why I said that. Just ignore me. I've been here all day, and I've had way too much blue food dye, both in cotton candy and blue raspberry snow cones. I wouldn't be surprised if I wake up tomorrow with blue skin. Now I'm even talking silly."

I squeezed her hand back. "Go home, Lauren. I'll let you know if I find out anything more. After all, this is your story," I reminded her. "You're covering the fair."

"But you were following the Rupert Madison court case." She sat forward and twisted toward me. "Do you think this had to do with the court case? Maybe it was that farmer, the man trying so hard to dunk Rupert this morning."

"It's a big jump from throwing a softball at a dunk booth and shooting someone dead, but I'm sure this'll be figured out soon."

Lauren's face lit up as she looked past me. "I'm sure it will. Detective Jackson just arrived."

My pulse raced. "Jackson is here?" I asked.

Lauren looked puzzled. "Yes, why are you squeezing my hand so hard? Is something up between you?"

I let go of her hand. "Oops, sorry. Uh, no, nothing wrong. I'm a little on edge after the long day. Why don't you head home, Lauren. And drink some water. You wouldn't look good in blue."

She laughed as she picked her backpack up off the ground. "Hello, Detective Jackson," she called and waved. "I'll let you have your partner back now."

I forced a grin. "See you tomorrow, Lauren." I stayed in one position, faced away from Jackson, for a few more seconds. I took a deep breath, stood up and turned. My heart sank. Jackson was already walking across the grass toward the murder scene. He never even said hello.

CHAPTER 16

My heart heavy, I considered, for all of a minute, leaving the park. It wasn't my job to investigate a murder. That burden fell to Detective Jackson. But I'd spent a good part of my work week following the victim around as he angered one person after another. I was too much a part of the case to walk away.

It wasn't easy, but I stiffened my backbone, along with my resolve, and strolled with purpose toward where the officials were huddled. One of the officers was debriefing Jackson, but I wasn't sure how much information he had to relay. I was sure I had far more in my journalist's notebook than the officer had in his. But that was Jackson's problem. If he couldn't be bothered to even acknowledge my presence, especially after Lauren made a big show of it, then I couldn't be bothered to fill him in on the details I'd gathered in my reporting.

The Higgins lawsuit was fairly common knowledge, but did Jackson know Higgins had been at the fair this morning, determined to soak his nemesis in the dunk tank? Did he know Veronica Blaine and her group of disgruntled homeowners attended both the court trial and movie night to shout out protests to the victim? Not only that, but Veronica had dated Rupert in the past. I was certain Jackson had no idea Madison, rudely and without proper cause, fired a young man for something as mundane as an apple core. Or that the same young man had also eagerly stepped up to dunk Madison in the tank. And what about the wife who'd packed up the kids and moved to Hawaii? As I mentally listed everything I knew, I realized I had my work cut out for me.

The victim was surrounded by officials. I would no longer have access to the crime scene, especially since the detective and I were not on speaking terms. When did that happen? We'd had arguments and cooling off periods before, but this felt far too real.

An empty popcorn container rolled into my foot, startling me from my thoughts. (Probably a good thing.) I bent over and picked up the container with the intention of throwing it away. I looked around for a trash can and realized that the entire area was covered with litter. Deborah had politely asked people to clean up after themselves, but the frantic ending to the evening caused most people to leave quickly and in shock. The cleanup crew never made it onto the field before the police cleared the area.

I picked up a few other pieces of trash in my vicinity and carried them to a large trash bin adjacent to the popcorn machine. There were still popped kernels in the heated center of the machine. They were starting to smell like burned popcorn. I searched around for a switch but couldn't find one, so I bent down and pulled the plug from the extension cord. The entire movie night had been frozen in time. Trash fluttered amongst the seats, uneaten popcorn was piled in the cart and the victim's face floated around on empty candy bar wrappers.

A few of the officers began walking back and forth through

the rows of chairs. As much as I tried to avoid looking at him, Jackson's height and overall presence was impossible to ignore. He was on the phone, presumably talking to the coroner. I knew one person on his contact list he wasn't calling. Me. As he spoke, he glanced around the park. I told myself he wasn't looking for me, but his visual search ended abruptly when his gaze landed on me. I turned away quickly. As I moved, my shin smacked the open cabinet door on the popcorn cart. I rubbed my leg and pushed shut the door. Something was keeping it from latching. I pulled it open and straightened in surprise.

There was always something shocking and off-putting about seeing a gun. Jackson wore one most of the time, but it was always tucked deep in his leather shoulder holster. All I ever saw was the backend, the grip as they called it in official circles. It was far less intimidating than seeing the whole thing, butt to barrel. And a gun looked especially out of place inside the cabinet of a brightly-colored popcorn cart. My big dilemma was how to let the police know what I'd found without having to speak directly to the detective in charge. Why couldn't they have sent out Detective Willow? He tended to be slower and less effective as an investigator, but there was one big advantage. He wasn't my boyfriend. Detective Willow had a wife, children and grandchildren, all of whom he loved talking about when given the opportunity. It would have been much easier to listen to one of his stories about his grandson's baseball game or his granddaughter's dance recital than to work up the courage to talk to Jackson.

At the same time, why not? Why not show Jackson how invaluable I was on these cases by letting him know I'd found the murder weapon. While his team was sifting through candy wrappers and spilled popcorn, I'd found the piece of evidence that might very well crack the case.

It took far more *courage* than I'd imagined to walk across to the crime scene. When Jackson turned my direction some of it crumbled. I slowed my pace. His gaze held mine as I willed my feet to keep moving toward him. The same hurt I was feeling deep down was reflected in his face. But this wasn't the time or place to discuss our relationship.

"Detective Jackson," I said in the coolest, calmest tone I could muster, "I think I've found the murder weapon." All attention snapped my direction. I hesitantly pointed my thumb over my shoulder. I hadn't expected everyone to look at me, and I was thrown off. "It's inside the cabinet on the popcorn cart."

Jackson's amber gaze glittered with what seemed like pride, then he pulled it away. "Officer Martinez, take an evidence bag and collect the weapon. Take a photo first," he added as the officer headed toward the cart.

"Thank you, Miss Taylor," Jackson said quietly. His shoulders lifted with a deep breath. He pulled away from the circle of yellow tape and headed across to where I was standing. The last bits of courage melted completely when he got close enough that I could smell his soap and aftershave.

He didn't say anything at first. We both stood in awkward silence for a long moment until he finally spoke. "You were at the movie," he said.

"Yes."

"What do you think happened? It seems unusual for a man to get shot dead in the middle of a movie with a lot of people sitting around him." We were going to talk about the crime. That was for the best.

I glanced over at the chair where Rupert had been sitting. His body had been moved to the grass next to the chair, waiting for the coroner's arrival. "He was sitting near the far end and the rear of the seating area. The movie—well, there's that loud gunfight at the end." He was nodding as I spoke. Jackson and I were always thinking on the same wavelength. "The noise—"

"The shooter was able to hide the sound of the gun because so many shots were being fired on-screen."

I pointed out all the speakers. "It was loud."

"Good detective work," he added.

"Detective Jackson, the coroner has arrived," an officer called.

"Right." Jackson turned back to me for a second. His mouth opened slightly as if he wanted to say something. Then he closed it and gazed at me for a moment before walking away. A little chunk of my soul went with him.

It had been a long day. Nothing sounded better than a shower and bed.

CHAPTER 17

My refrigerator was disappointingly empty. That didn't stop me from opening it, not once or twice but three times, in case I missed something like a freshly baked coffee cake or a ready-to-heat frittata hiding behind the carton of milk or the half-eaten sandwich that was far past its prime. Unfortunately, there were no hidden goodies. Even my loaf of bread was down to dry heels. At least there was coffee to brew.

I'd finished my story early and found myself with some spare time. I contemplated starting that novel I'd always wanted to write, but I had no characters, no plot and, if I was being honest, no particular genre selected. The whole idea was only a whisper in my brain telling me I should write a novel. Someday, maybe. I was hardly in a state of mind or emotion to be creative.

I started up the coffee maker and sat at the table to stare absently out the window. I loved the view from the kitchen in the morning. Clusters of wildflowers swayed in the breeze. They were the last of the summer colors before the golds and reds of autumn took over. Redford and Newman had gone outside first thing. They'd found a stick long enough to play tug-of-war.

Newman's ball chasing skills made him the stronger, more cunning of the two. Poor Redford couldn't keep a grip on the stick. Newman snatched the prize and ran off with Redford bounding behind to win it back.

"No breakfast?" Edward appeared in front of me. I could still see my dogs playing through his transparent waistcoat.

"Turns out my refrigerator doesn't have an automatic refill button."

Edward's brow cocked in question.

"I didn't go to the store. The cupboards are bare."

"I see. Perhaps Brady will arrive with those big sausage shaped monstrosities that drip sauce and onions."

"Hmm, a breakfast burrito does sound tasty. But he's not coming."

Edward moved closer to the table. He stared down at me with his intense blue gaze. "Is this still about the elephant?" he asked.

A laugh spilled from my mouth. I looked up at him. "You do know there is no actual elephant, right?"

Edward's face dropped. "I've concluded that I'm the elephant. Couldn't I have been compared to something a little more imposing, like a horse or a wolfhound?"

"Sorry, elephant is the one that works in this situation." I looked at him and sighed. "Jackson and I have been planning a future together."

"Yes, he showed me the plans for his barn. I'm the one that suggested he add more windows. Animals can get sick if they don't get adequate fresh air."

I stared at him again. "When did you two have *that* conversation?"

Edward moved back as the two dogs came bounding through the dog door. "Last week when he was here working on that loud machine."

"See, that's what I don't understand." I got up. I was going to need coffee for the rest of this conversation because I was now not just hungry but irritated as well. "I've walked in on the two of you having civil, even, dare I say, friendly conversations about things you have in common, like horses and barns." I poured a cup of coffee. The aroma alone gave me a shot of energy. "As soon as you add me into the mix, the two of you start arguing and throwing insults like two siblings. Why is that?"

Edward drifted toward his favorite place on the hearth. "I don't know what you're talking about. We simply engage in lively banter."

"No, banter implies something fun and teasing. Sometimes it starts that way but then it builds to this annoying, aggravating crescendo. Then, I have to step in like a scolding fishwife—"

Edward laughed. "You are hardly a fishwife, though you do tend to lean toward scolding."

"See, not usually." I carried my cup across to the fireplace. Edward had the advantage of being everywhere all at once. I needed to be standing for this conversation and not glued to one spot at the kitchen table. "I'm normally easy-going, carefree, at least until you—" I'd made a misstep. I'd learned long ago never to point out to Edward how much his presence impacted my life. There was nothing he could do about it, and that always left him depressed.

"Until I interrupted your life," he added darkly.

"No, I interrupted yours," I reminded him. "And it's fine. I've grown inexplicably fond of having you as part of my life." His image cleared up, a sure sign that my words helped. "I need to understand why the two of you get so bristled by each other and why I seem to be the catalyst."

Edward floated off toward the window. I'd made the right call by staying mobile. I followed him. He hadn't expected it. "Why are you at my heels?"

"Because I want an answer."

His image faded.

"Don't erase yourself, pal. I need to know. My future with Jackson depends on this. I don't even know if there is a future."

His face came back fully. He was so handsome sometimes, like now, when his features were crystal clear, I could easily imagine Edward in the flesh standing in front of me. I was sure Kathy, the woman he loved, must have gotten caught up in his magnetic blue gaze many times.

"If he leaves you, he's a bigger fool than I imagined. And I imagined quite a lot."

"Stop avoiding the question. Why is it the two of you act civilized toward each other when I'm not there to witness it?"

A long, dramatic pause followed. I wasn't sure how long it felt in ghost time, but for me, it seemed long enough that I wasn't going to get an answer. I was about to give up when he spoke.

"Perhaps, we're both contrary with each other because we're both vying for the same person's love and attention."

I had so many follow-up questions, but they stuck in my throat. Raine teased me constantly about Edward being in love with me. Even Jackson had brought it up, but it was so implausible, I never gave any of it much credence.

"Edward." His name came out on a shocked whisper. A knock was followed by the front door opening and shutting. Edward vanished.

"Yoo hoo," Emily called as she headed toward the kitchen. The dogs, exhausted from their morning of play, managed to get up from their pillows to greet the woman carrying an aroma-filled basket. "I heard there was another dead body, so I figured I'd head over here to find out what was going on." She stopped in the doorway of the kitchen and crinkled her nose. "Is that what happens after one crosses into their thirties—gossip becomes a focal point of the day?" She lifted the basket. "I also brought you some of my savory mustard and cheddar cheese muffins."

MOVIE NIGHT MADNESS

I hadn't recovered completely from the last few moments with Edward. It took me a second to decipher everything Emily said. The muffins grabbed my attention the most.

"You're officially my angel on earth. I have nothing in the refrigerator. Coffee?"

"No, thanks. I've already had three cups today. I practically skipped all the way here." She placed the basket on the table.

I grabbed two plates from the cupboard and sat across from her. Emily's flawless skin was pink from the brisk walk over. I plucked a plump, cheesy muffin from the basket and set it on a plate. "It's as if you were reading my mind."

"Was I right with the rest of the mind reading? Was my sister at the scene of another murder?" Her blue eyes sparkled with anticipation. It was the three cups of coffee.

"Yes, you were right about that too."

"I knew it." She clapped loudly enough that Newman startled. "Oops. I really need to switch to decaf. I heard it was Rupert Madison, the rich developer. Someone shot him dead during the movie."

I swallowed a delicious bite of muffin. "Sounds like you know as much as me."

"Oh, come on. Don't be a tease. How did he get shot in the middle of a crowded movie night?"

"I think they used the shootout in the movie to cover up the noise. No one noticed because of the gunfire."

Emily picked at one of her muffins. "Then it must have been someone who knew the movie well enough to plan their murder at the right time."

"Good point, Em. Although, the movie is a classic, and the end scene is sort of a classic right along with it."

Emily twisted her lip in thought. "I don't think I've ever seen it."

My eyes rounded. "Is that even possible? I assumed everyone

had seen it multiple times. I suppose your age group might have missed out on some of the big classics."

"Guess that counts out anyone in my *age* group as a suspect."

"Not necessarily."

"Is Jackson on the case?" she asked before another nibble. Emily cooked so much good food, but she was still a nibbler, like she was growing up. She loved food and was a great judge of whether something was good or not, but she never ate with the same gusto as Lana and me. It was annoying.

My phone beeped with a text. It was Jackson. I had to play it cool and be very nonchalant about the text or my sister would suspect something was up. My insides were churning with nerves, but I stayed calm on the outside. Not an easy feat. I swiped my finger across to open the text.

"Since you found the murder weapon, I thought you might be interested to know the gun was registered to Boris Rossdale. He's a Firefly local. I'm heading into a meeting, then I'm driving out to talk to him." That was the end of the text. It was business-like and brief. There was no flirty comment at the end. At least he'd decided to keep me in the loop. I was grateful and, at the same time, confused. The whole morning was, once again, turning into an emotional roller coaster.

"Was that Jax?" Emily asked.

"Yes. I found the murder weapon last night. Now they have a name connected to it. Boris Rossdale."

Emily sat up straighter. "Boris Rossdale? I know his wife, Felicity. She buys my eggs. She's one of those big yard sale junkies. She buys stuff, fixes it and then holds her own yard sale and online auction to sell her salvaged goods. Makes a pretty penny with it too. Boris is a retired mailman. I wonder what connection he could possibly have with Rupert Madison."

"I'm not sure, but I know how to find out." I lifted a brow. "Exactly where do the Rossdales live?"

CHAPTER 18

I hurried along my visit with Emily to get back on the case. If there was one thing I could always count on to get my mind off my woes, it was a murder investigation. Emily had once purchased an antique pie safe from Felicity Rossdale, so she knew they lived a block past the Firefly Junction Fire Station in a red brick house with white columns, a white portico and a rose garden.

Her description led me right to the house. A dozen or so plum, pink and yellow rose bushes were bursting with late summer color in the front yard. A big, erasable yard sale sign was tucked into the shrubs on the left side of the house. Last weekend's date was handwritten on the bottom.

I headed up the steps to the front door, a heavily varnished mahogany masterpiece with paneling and a leaded glass window across the top. A brass lion's head held the door knocker in its mouth. I picked up the brass ring and knocked twice. A car pulled around the corner to the Rossdale's quiet, tree-lined street.

A new surge of adrenaline again, all courtesy of Detective Jackson. He wouldn't be pleased to see me. Maybe he had two reasons to be displeased. Edward's comment had certainly left me baffled and speechless. Emily's visit had cut short our talk. I hoped we could pick it up again, but there were no guarantees with Edward. Sometimes, he was in the mood to share his feelings, and sometimes, he could clam up as tightly as a... well, a clam.

The door opened as Jackson got out of his car. The woman behind the door was forty-ish with bright orange hair that was teased up high. She had orange lipstick to match her hair. "If this is about the antique buffet, another woman bought it this morning. You should have messaged me. I could have saved you the trip." She was about to close the door when she spotted Jackson walking up the pathway. "Now, who's this?"

Jackson heard the question and had his badge ready. "I'm Detective Jackson and this is—" He paused and looked at me. "This is my assistant, Miss Taylor."

I was a jumbled mix of relief, surprise and glee.

"A detective? What's this about?"

"We're here to talk to Boris Rossdale," Jackson explained.

"Boris? Yes, that's my husband. Just a moment." She walked away without letting us in. She left the door slightly ajar, apparently not wanting to be rude by closing a door in a detective's face. Her departure left Jackson and me with a moment alone.

"Thank you for telling her I was your assistant."

"You're the one that found the gun." He pretended to be interested in the front yard and rose garden as he looked everywhere but directly at me. I wasn't going to waste the opportunity to find out exactly what was on his mind.

"Are we ever going to discuss our elephant problem?" I asked bluntly. "Or have you given up on us?" The second question surprised both of us. I hadn't expected to lob the grenade. It just came out.

His gaze pulled back to my face. "I'm not giving up on us.

Never, Bluebird." The rush of emotion I felt hearing him call me Bluebird was hard to hide. "I'm just not sure if there's a solution to the elephant problem."

Felicity returned to the door. A man in his late fifties or early sixties, mostly bald with a heavy moustache and deep-set eyes, appeared at the door looking more than a little worried.

"Detective Jackson? I'm Boris Rossdale." He opened the door wider, shook Jackson's hand and waved us into the house. "Please, come inside."

We stepped into a small entryway with a blue and white checked tile floor and an antique chandelier dripping with crystal hanging from the ceiling. Boris shut the door. "What can I do for you, Detective?" Boris looked fleetingly at me but spoke directly to Jackson.

"Mr. Rossdale, were you at the end-of-summer fair at the park yesterday?"

Rossdale looked stunned by the question. "Yes, yes I was. I love the corndogs on a stick. I wait every year for them to come back. No crime in that I hope." He added in a nervous laugh.

"No crime in eating a corndog. Did you stay for the movie?"

"Felicity and I planned to go to the movie, but she developed a headache."

Felicity touched her temple. "I get terrible migraines. We had to cancel our plans. I went to bed early."

"Where were you between ten and eleven o'clock last night, Mr. Rossdale?"

His moustache twitched nervously. "I was right here. When my wife is suffering from one of her bad headaches, I sleep out on the couch. I don't like to disturb her."

She smiled at him. "He's always considerate like that."

I wasn't getting any murder vibes from Boris Rossdale, but what did I know? I was just the assistant.

"You may have heard there was an incident last night. A man was shot at movie night," Jackson said.

Felicity's hand went to her chest. "I saw some online chatter about Rupert Madison being dead. I thought it was just rumors."

"I'm afraid not. Mr. Rossdale, the reason I'm—we're here is that Rupert Madison was shot."

Rossdale's mouth dropped open. "My goodness. In the middle of a crowd? How is that possible?"

"We have our theories." Jackson wasn't going to get into details. He had one purpose for the visit, but I sensed he was getting the same non-murderer vibes as me. Some of the tension that went with a possible arrest had disappeared from his shoulders and posture. "Mr. Rossdale, I'll get right to the point. We found a gun at the park that has been matched to the bullet that killed Mr. Madison."

Felicity was still in her pearl-clutching routine. "That poor, poor man."

"I see," Mr. Rossdale said with a look that showed he clearly didn't.

"The gun, a Glock 19, was registered to you."

Boris's face drained of color. It took him a second to find his words. "That's impossible. I have a gun. My brother insisted I should buy one for protection, but I hated having the thing in the house. I keep it inside a suitcase. I've been looking at gun safes, but they're so expensive."

Jackson's head tilted. "I don't understand. You store it outside? In a suitcase?"

I had to agree—it seemed like a careless place to leave a gun.

"It's not outside. It's in the garage, up in the rafters. I'll show you." Jackson and I followed Boris out of the house. Felicity scooted along on house slippers behind us.

"I had no idea you owned a gun," Felicity said as we reached a two-car garage. "You know you should never listen to Morton.

Remember the stock in that crazy vacuum company? 'The next big thing in house vacuums,' Morty claimed. It was all a sham." Felicity continued. Boris was doing a good job ignoring her comments. Something told me it was a skill he practiced a lot.

Boris pulled a set of keys from his trouser pocket and unlocked the side door of the garage. "I'm sure this is all a mistake. That suitcase hasn't left this garage in a year."

"That's because you don't take me anywhere," Felicity added.

This time Boris shot her an aggravated scowl as he lifted a three-tiered stepladder off a hook. He carried it over to the center of the garage and stared up at the rafters. Boxes, a giant Santa cutout and a dusty pair of skis hung overhead.

"Now, where is that suitcase," Boris muttered as he shifted the stepladder around. We had our faces turned up toward the rafters, but there was no sign of a suitcase.

"It's light blue with travel stickers plastered on the sides," Boris noted.

"That one?" Felicity asked. "The one you got from your sister?"

"Yes, that's it." Boris looked up again. "Do you see it?"

Felicity grew quiet. She pressed her fingers to her lips for a second. "I sold it at the yard sale. I didn't know it had a gun inside of it," she added quickly. "You never told me you bought a gun. I think that's something a wife should know." She looked at me for support. I nodded in agreement. Unfortunately, proving her point wasn't going to help the fact that she sold a suitcase with a Glock 19 to some unsuspecting yard sale shopper.

"I don't need to tell you how serious this is," Jackson noted. "Next time you decide to arm yourself, spend the money on a safe."

Boris looked properly chastised. His face dropped. "Yes, Detective Jackson. I've learned that lesson now." Something occurred to him. "My gun was used to murder Rupert Madison?"

His face drained of color, and he wiped beads of sweat off his forehead with the back of his hand. "Felicity, who bought that suitcase?" he asked.

Felicity folded her bottom lip in and rolled up her eyes in thought. "Let me think. Light blue suitcase," she said to herself. "Light blue suitcase," she repeated. "Nope, can't remember."

"Mrs. Rossdale, this is important," Jackson said.

"Yes, for goodness sake, Felicity. Think, dear."

She repeated the lip and eye roll and still came up empty-headed. "It was a well-attended yard sale. I must have had a hundred people walk through, and *you* were watching the baseball game, so I was on my own. It was hectic. I'm sorry, Detective Jackson. I can't remember who bought it. But I'll call you if it comes to me."

Jackson's shoulders dropped in disappointment. "Please do. Before I leave, one more question, Mr. Rossdale."

"Yes, of course. Anything."

"Did you know Rupert Madison or have any business dealings with him?"

"Me? No. We traveled in very different circles. I spend my days playing golf and watching television. I've never even met the man."

Jackson nodded. "Please, call me if you remember anything about the suitcase."

Boris led us to the door. "Absolutely. And don't worry. I've certainly learned my lesson about gun ownership."

We walked out of the garage. Awkwardness had returned. We were no longer investigating a murder. For those few seconds, we were two people, alone, returning to our cars. My heart sank when those few seconds ended with Jackson's short words. "We'll talk later." He didn't even walk me to my Jeep.

CHAPTER 19

Another morning where my emotions ran the length of the spectrum. I was quietly thrilled when Jackson introduced me as his assistant. He could have just as easily dismissed me, telling me to leave so he could move along with official business. Letting me stay was a big deal. It also gave me hope that all this would blow over easily. His curt farewell brought me back down to earth. He'd allowed me to stay as payment of sorts for finding the weapon, but that was the end of our *partnership* on the investigation.

If only Boris Rossdale had been the killer, then the case could be tied up quickly and I could earn credit for finding a major piece of evidence. The murder weapon could have ended up in anyone's hands. The suspect list had just grown to epic proportions. Fortunately, my article on Madison gave me some solid places to start. Veronica Blaine was on the top of my list.

I made myself a cup of hot tea and sat at the table with my laptop. I'd only had a few brief interactions with Veronica, but I already had a good sense of her character. Did that sense lead me to believe she was a murderer? Not necessarily. But she was absolutely someone who got involved in community issues. That led to my next conclusion, one I easily verified by pulling up the neighbor app on my computer. As expected, Veronica Blaine was a frequent poster and commenter. She was not afraid to speak her mind. (I wasn't sure if that was a good or bad quality, but it was definitely a quality.)

It only took a short time perusing past posts to see that Veronica was highly critical of every aspect of Rupert Madison's life. She wrote that the town would someday be consumed by Madison's big dirt movers, leaving behind only paved parking lots and empty shop fronts. One thread had forty comments about problems people were having with their Madison homes. Someone even *graciously* posted photographic proof of a backed-up toilet, a visual aid I could have done without.

I scrolled through to Veronica's most recent post. She was hosting a community meeting at the recreation center in her neighborhood. The meeting was at two o'clock today. It was going to be easier than I thought to talk to Veronica Blaine. She'd had a nervous, agitated reaction to Rupert's murder. I was interested to find out what her feelings were about the tragedy. Did she consider it a tragedy? Did the homeowners have to drop their lawsuit now that the defendant was dead? They could take on his trust or his company, but that would take an entirely new filing. The homeowners would likely not get results for years, if at all.

"You seem distracted," Edward said.

I didn't look up from the screen. I rarely went on the neighborhood app, but when I did drop by, I always found something interesting. Someone in the next neighborhood over was giving away feed troughs. I marked down the information. I still had an audience. It was strange how noticeable Edward's presence was even though he wasn't in solid form.

"I'm working on a murder case," I said. "A man died last night at the outdoor movie in the park. Shot dead."

He swept closer. "You could have been harmed," he said frantically.

"But I wasn't." I lifted out both arms to show I was in one piece.

"Why are you investigating the case? Isn't there a local detective to do the work?"

"You know there is. But I prefer to get to the bottom of things myself."

Edward put on what I referred to as his brooding ghost expression. "I don't like it."

"You don't like what?" I asked.

"You, gallivanting around town chasing down people with guns."

I got up to put my cup in the sink. "Then, lucky for me, you have no say in the matter. I am an entirely independent woman." I winked at him. "We're like that now, liberated, free from the Victorian patriarchy. We even show our ankles with wild abandon." I waved toward my legs, clad only in shorts and sandals.

"You needn't remind me of that. I don't eat or sleep, but I can see quite well."

"Good, with that discussion over, I'm off for a day of gallivanting. With any luck, I'll catch a killer."

Edward looked truly crestfallen. It bothered him to no end that he couldn't follow me around to protect me. It was annoying but sweet.

"Edward, thanks for worrying about me. I'll be careful."

He bowed his head. "You'll have to be. That wild-haired descendant of mine does a poor job of watching out for your well-being."

I groaned. "And the elephant keeps on growing." I walked to the table to close my laptop and noticed something interesting. In the short time that I'd been extolling my independence someone had deleted all of Veronica Blaine's posts. I scrolled through some of the older ones. They all said deleted by the author. Veronica had decided to take down her negative comments about Rupert Madison. Was that out of respect for the dead? I doubted it. Maybe she worried her posts would lead the police to her doorstep as a viable suspect. Seemed starting with Veronica had been a good call.

CHAPTER 20

Other than a few dogs barking intermittently, Veronica Blaine's neighborhood was quiet. It looked much like every other newly built community. There were several styles of houses, and each style repeated itself three times on the same block. Paint colors and landscaping were the only things that made them different. Like with any neighborhood, some people kept neatly trimmed hedges and flower gardens, while others let the lawns turn a summery brown and kept their landscaping, in general, to a minimum.

The recreation center, community pool and tennis courts were in a central location. Several women were carrying foil covered trays into the squat plaster building. It had three big windows in the front, with shades pulled down to keep the sunlight from blazing through.

There was only one other car in the lot as I pulled in. Two men were at the pool with their kids. They splashed and screamed in the water. We'd had the end-of-summer fair, but there were still a few days of hot summer to be enjoyed. I always knew good times were over when our mom piled us into her car to go to the store for new shoes. I loved shopping as a kid (much more than I enjoy it now) but school shopping was always a depressing adventure. Late night sleepovers, swim parties and barbecues—all the things that made summer the best season of the year—would slowly disappear to be replaced by new, uncomfortable shoes, homework and book reports. I did, however, always look forward to a new year of playing sports.

I'd gotten to the event center fifteen minutes early hoping I could get a few words alone with Veronica. She was talking to several neighbors when I poked my head into the building. I stepped inside and headed to the back row of seats to wait for her to finish. A woman I recognized as a fellow court and movie night protester was pulling bakery cookies out of boxes and placing them on a platter. I walked over to her.

"Hello, I'm Sunni Taylor with the *Junction Times*."

The woman smiled. She had a sunburned face that showed where her sunglasses had been the day before. "Yes, of course. I loved your article on the new bird-watching craze. Even bought myself a pair of binoculars and a bird guide."

"Great. Glad to inspire. I was wondering—were you at movie night last night?" I was sure I'd seen her but needed to make certain.

Her entire face dropped to a frown. "Yes," she said somberly. "Such a shock and a tragedy. It's getting so no one is safe anymore. Who'd expect something like that to happen in the middle of movie night? Veronica had mentioned that she wanted us to take a fieldtrip to a shooting range. She thinks it's a smart idea to learn how to defend ourselves. She's in charge of the neighborhood watch." She laughed lightly. "Veronica's in charge of everything. I don't know where she gets the energy." Her frown had disappeared now that she'd launched into a sermon about how dangerous the world was and how important it was to protect ourselves. She seemed to be under the impression that

Madison had been an unlucky, random victim. Was that the case? I hadn't even considered that. It was highly unlikely considering only Madison was struck and definitively so. The person who shot Madison knew what they were doing.

"You said Veronica wants to take everyone to a shooting range? I take it she's a skilled shooter."

"She is humble about it, but she's very skilled. Her dad was a military man. He taught her everything she knows. It's a good skill to have, I'm sure, but to be honest, guns kind of freak me out. I told my husband we just need a really big dog. I much prefer that mode of protection."

"You can't hug a gun," I added.

She laughed. "See, that's just what I told Allen, my husband. He replied with—" She lifted her chest, dropped her chin and made her voice sound weirdly low. "Yes, but you don't have to clean up gun poop from the yard."

It was my turn to laugh. "Touché, Allen."

More people were filing into the building. It was amazing how many people could show up in the middle of the day, in the middle of the week. I was sure people wanted to attend to find out what would happen with the lawsuit.

Veronica spotted me at the back table. She walked my direction as she waited for people to find their seats. "Miss Taylor, right?"

"Yes, hello. I thought I'd drop by and find out what was happening with the HOA after yesterday's tragedy."

She worked hard at trying to look grim about it, but she wasn't fooling this reporter. Now that I knew about her expertise with guns, I was more than a little interested in talking to her.

"You should probably take your seat, Micah. We're going to start soon."

Micah smiled politely at me and hurried toward the rows of metal folding chairs. They were filling up fast.

"Looks like we're going to have a packed house," Veronica noted. "People want to know what will happen now that Madison is dead. Naturally, we've already put a great deal of time and money into the lawsuit. Most of us have spent hours compiling lists of problems we've had to deal with due to shoddy workmanship and Madison's corner cutting. Did you get the list I sent you?"

I'd seen it in my email, but I hadn't opened it yet. The article I'd submitted to Prudence was no longer going to work. Too much had changed in a matter of twenty-four hours.

"I haven't read through it yet, but I must tell you if you're continuing with the lawsuit—"

She straightened almost as if I'd insulted her. "Of course, we are. Someone needs to compensate us. If not Madison, then his company. And Mr. Lang's construction company, as well." In the flurry of activity, I'd forgotten about the contractor, Curtis Lang. He'd had to deal with the complaints about the workmanship. In the end, Madison overlooked Lang's company for the building of the shopping center. Was the center still going up? That seemed doubtful.

"That all makes sense, which is why I won't give out specific complaints in my article. I don't want to interfere with an ongoing legal case."

Her mouth pursed showing she was disappointed, but she nodded in agreement. "Thank you."

"You were at the movie last night. I saw you with your friends. Everyone looked very shocked about Madison's death."

Again, she straightened as if insulted. "Of course, we were shocked. Why wouldn't we be?"

"You're right. That was a clumsy observation. Did you talk to Madison at all before the movie?"

"No, we don't speak."

"I heard somewhere that the two of you once dated."

This time her reaction was almost as if someone had slapped her. "Who told you that?"

"It was just something I heard."

She looked around to make sure no one could hear our conversation. The acoustics in the building were terrible, and the other conversations all bounced off the walls and ceilings. It was too loud to hear anyone who wasn't directly next to you. "We dated temporarily. Back when the neighborhood was being built. Back before I knew what a greedy cheat Rupert was. I was glad to get away from him."

"You broke it off with him?"

She crossed her arms defensively and wriggled in her snug dress. "Naturally. I'm not sure where this conversation is going. Please do not mention my brief relationship with Rupert in your column. You do not have my permission to mention it."

"I won't." I didn't actually need her permission, but it was also not nearly intriguing enough to include. Unless, of course, Veronica was the killer.

"Your friend, Micah, is frightened after last night's shooting. She mentioned you were going to take interested HOA members to a shooting range for practice."

"Everyone is quite upset about it. The world is not a safe place. Madison's death has pushed a lot more people to sign up for the trip to the shooting range." The crowd grew bigger and louder. "I need to get the meeting started."

"Of course. Thank you for taking the time to talk to me."

Veronica hurried away clapping to get everyone's attention. She'd certainly made a point of walking over to talk to me. Was she someone who liked to see her name in the paper, or was there another motive? Was she interested in finding out what the nosy reporter was up to? I was sure she saw me on movie night and, more importantly, at the murder scene. Maybe Veronica Blaine wanted to make sure I wasn't nosing around about the murder she committed. It was too early to tell if that was the case, but she was certainly high on my list. I wondered how the actual detective's list was shaping up. Not too long ago, like last week, I could have merely texted the detective to find out what was happening with the investigation.

I sighed dejectedly as I left the building. Behind me, Veronica was calling the meeting to order. I supposed it made sense that they would continue with the lawsuit. Madison's death didn't correct the wrongs that had been made. The opposite, in fact. His death was going to make compensation a lot more difficult. That brought me back to the question of motive. Why would Veronica kill him if his death was a major setback for the lawsuit? Unless it was a crime of passion?

CHAPTER 21

Curtis Lang's construction company office was located in Birch Highlands. I'd talked to Veronica. Now, it was time to talk to my second suspect. I'd never met Curtis. I'd heard about him from Veronica Blaine. She was not a fan because Curtis had been the contractor for her neighborhood. Madison had Curtis cutting corners, allegedly. If that was the case, why did Curtis go along with it? If he had any integrity as a contractor, he would have refused to cut corners and leave homeowners with shabby workmanship. That didn't seem to be the case. Even though Curtis had to deal with the stress of multiple complaints and a pending lawsuit, he supposedly sought a new contract with Madison for the shopping center. The headaches left behind from the house debacle hadn't tainted his opinion of Madison enough to make him avoid working with the developer again. That, to me, signaled a man who not only lacked integrity but who was greedy enough to risk his reputation and that of his company for financial gain. Did that also make him a killer? According to what seemed like relevant sources, Madison turned down Lang's bid for the shopping center. That couldn't have made Lang very happy, considering all the trouble Madison had brought down on his head. Did he feel that Madison owed him?

The construction office was situated in the middle of a small industrial park. Work trucks and earth moving equipment were parked next to the building. A huge workshop with a roll-up door cast a wide shadow over the small office. I parked my Jeep. There was a light on in the office, but I didn't see anyone inside.

I got out and walked up to the door and was greeted with a *Closed* sign. A loud bang startled me. I swung around. A man wearing a shirt with the Lang logo on the pocket was piling rebar into a work truck.

He wiped his forehead with the back of his hand, then wiped his hands off on his work pants. "Can I help you?"

"I was looking for Mr. Lang."

"Are you a supplier? Deliveries are between noon and four."

"I'm not delivering anything. I was hoping to talk to him."

He looked at me skeptically. "Are you with the police?"

My eyes rounded. "No. Should I be?"

"Don't know. Lang travels around during the day, stopping at worksites. You won't have much luck catching him here at the office."

"Do you have the addresses of those worksites? I'm with the *Junction Times*." It was time to flash the press pass. Sometimes the pass made people more friendly, more receptive. Occasionally, it had the opposite effect. Unfortunately, his reaction was the latter.

"Can't give those to you." His expression grew sterner, and he returned to his task. He lifted a huge load of rebar, swung the long, bouncy bars around and shoved them into his truck. I stood there for a moment hoping he'd reconsider. He didn't.

"If this is about that cranky lady who's suing the boss because she had a few plaster cracks in her ceiling, then I've got nothing more to say."

"I have no idea who you're talking about," I said.

He peered up at me through a skeptical squint. "Right. And I'm an astronaut. This is just my side job."

"Fine, I know Veronica Blaine, and I know about the lawsuit, but she didn't send me."

He lifted another bundle of rebar and swung it around almost menacingly. I'd worn out my welcome.

"Thanks for your time," I said dryly. I spun around and startled as the rebar landed in the truck behind me. I was more than eager to get back to the Jeep. I wasn't giving up on talking to Lang, but his grumpy, overly suspicious, journalist-hating worker had been an unexpected obstacle.

I drove out of the lot and headed back toward town. I had a few destinations on my mental list. I was interested to find out if work was still in progress at Sunridge, Madison's latest neighborhood. As I drove along the main road through Birch Highlands, something, or, more accurately, someone caught my eye.

Detective Willow, the new detective the precinct had hired to help with the caseload was leaving the pharmacy with a small white bag. Roy Willow was a middle-aged man with crinkly, permanent smile lines around his gray eyes. He was also usually cheery, and that cheeriness transferred to the way he walked. But not today. He was moving exceptionally slow, and while one hand clutched the prescription bag, the other rested on his lower back. He looked distressed and wasn't wearing his usual smile.

I parked the Jeep. He was moving at such a slow pace it was easy to catch up to him. "Detective Willow," I called. It was difficult for him to look back, so I took fast steps and pulled up even with him. His usual smile returned, but he was working at it to be polite. A grimace of pain was behind it.

"Sunni, how nice to see you. It's a bright spot in an otherwise terrible day."

"Oh dear, have you hurt yourself?" I asked. We continued to

walk toward his car. Standing on the sidewalk took a lot of his energy.

"It's the most embarrassing, ridiculous thing. I got to the precinct this morning. As I was headed toward my desk, I threw away the wrapper from my breakfast sandwich. Blanche always makes me a special to-go breakfast when I'm off to work. This one had two soft egg patties and two slices of bacon. She puts a few jalapeño slices in when she's feeling devilish. So good." For a second, he forgot about his pain, and he was back with his yummy breakfast sandwich. "Anyhow, that darn piece of parchment didn't land in the can. I doubled back to pick it up and put it properly in the waste can, and darn, if I didn't throw out my back." He rubbed his back as he spoke. "It's an old high school football injury. Comes back to haunt me every once in a while. Sure didn't expect this. I'm afraid Jax is going to be busy this week. He's got to pick up my caseload too. I'm hoping a few days of muscle relaxers will do the trick. Gosh, I hope you two didn't have big plans this week. I hate to think I spoiled them with something as silly as bending over to pick up trash."

"No big plans." Of that I was certain. "Go home and rest. I hope you feel better soon."

"I will. Blanche is probably working on one of her smelly, gooey poultices right now."

We reached his car. "Do you happen to know how the Rupert Madison murder case is going?" I had time because it was taking him literally minutes just to step off the curb. "Is there something I can do to help you?"

"Only if you happen to have a crane in your back pocket that can lift me off this sidewalk and onto the road." He chuckled, then winced. "Guess laughing is out today as well. You probably know more about the case than me." He held his breath and finally took the step down off the curb. A few more deep breaths got him to the driver's side of the car. "See you later, Sunni."

"You too, Roy. Take care."

I waited to see that he got safely into his car. It was another full two minutes. I waved as he pulled away, then I headed back to my Jeep. Hopefully, my next stop would prove more fruitful than the first one.

CHAPTER 22

Surprisingly, or maybe not surprisingly, work continued on the Sunridge neighborhood. It made sense. Madison's company had obligations to fill. People had put deposits on new houses, and they were expecting them to be finished on time.

I parked at the end of the development where the new curbs and sidewalks ended. The community was surrounded by empty dirt lots. Madison probably owned most of the land and had most likely been planning to develop all of it. Higgins was right. When was it too much?

I had no invitation to tour the site like last time. That tour ended rather abruptly and with a tense exchange between me and my tour guide. A woman in a pencil skirt and shoes that were better left for a night out than a construction site was heading toward the model home with a young couple. They were wearing hardhats indicating they'd just taken a tour of the neighborhood. My guess was the woman was the realtor Madison employed to sell his Sunridge homes. Maybe she'd be the right person to talk to. She wasn't involved in the construction, but she might have some insider's information about Madison Homes. If Madison's wife and kids lived in Hawaii, someone else must have been second-in-charge at the company. Maybe that second-in-command had motive.

I headed toward the model home and stepped inside. "I'll be right with you," the woman called. She continued cataloguing all the wonderful features each house would come with, both standard and optional. Most of the good stuff, like tile in the bathrooms and a convection oven, were extras.

I wandered around pretending to be interested, all the while planning how to handle this. The last thing I wanted or had time for was to listen to a long sales pitch about a house I had no intention of buying. At the same time, another tour of the site might be beneficial. What I really wanted was to interview Jeremy Sexton's coworkers, the ones who witnessed his cold dismissal by the boss. A long sales pitch would be torturous, and I'd never get to ask any pertinent questions. I certainly didn't need to know if plush carpeting and sprinklers were optional. However, if I played my cards right... It took a lot of back and forth, but I finally made my decision. I slipped my press pass under my shirt and waited as the woman walked the young couple to the door, their hands filled with brochures, business cards and loan applications.

The second she closed the door, she tossed her sales smile my direction. "Hello, I'm Barbara. Welcome to the Sunridge Community."

"Sunni." I left off the last name in case she was a frequent reader of the *Junction Times*. "I heard the model was open." I glanced around the room. It was one of those big open space floor plans with a kitchen off to the side and a few windows looking out over a dirt backyard. "Very nice. Lots of room. Will they all look like this inside?" That question was to satisfy my curiosity. All the houses were similar on the outside. I wondered if the uniformity carried inside.

Barbara strode on her heels across the vinyl flooring to the kitchen island where the brochures were stacked. "Each style home has a similar layout, but room sizes vary depending on the model. How many bedrooms are you looking for? There are three and four bedroom models."

"Gosh, haven't given it much thought. Three, I guess."

She looked at my left hand. No ring on the finger. Maybe that would never happen now. I pushed that gloomy thought aside.

"Just you?" she asked.

"Uh, for now. I'm still in the research stage. I have to admit, I saw some bad reviews for Madison Homes online. A lot of unhappy customers."

She tugged sharply at her fitted coat. It was periwinkle blue over a black pencil skirt. "I'm only the realtor. The Madison Company hired me to sell the homes in this community. I have nothing to do with the construction."

"Yes, but don't you have a fiduciary duty to do what's best for the client?"

"Maybe you should take home a brochure and look it over." She stuck out a brochure. I was being dismissed and rather rudely. It seemed my usual finesse had been dampened by my stressful private life. I hated to think I drove out here to leave only with a brochure. I'd chosen the wrong tact and needed to start again.

"Look, of course, you're a realtor, and you had nothing to do with the construction. I'm just trying to gather as much information as I can about this development. Buying a house is a big decision, and I want to make sure I'm not making the wrong choice." I moved a little closer. "It's a weird coincidence, but on my way here, I was listening to a local station. The DJ mentioned that Rupert Madison had been shot at the Firefly Junction movie night."

The fake sales-pitch face cracked, and a more somber expres-

MOVIE NIGHT MADNESS

sion appeared. "Yes, it's just awful." Her perfect posture melted, and she seemed relieved to be able to talk about it. "The police don't know who did it. Rupert Madison could be a cutthroat businessman and a hard person to work for, but he didn't deserve that. His family is returning today. I'm sure they are devastated."

"Returning?" I asked, pretending to be clueless.

"His wife and children lived—well, they didn't live with Rupert. I think there were some family problems. He never spoke about it, but I believe they were separated."

"His company was so big and successful. Who takes over now?"

"No one seems to know. Rupert liked to run things on his own. He had a few upper management people, now and then, but because he never liked to let go of the reins most of those people moved on. It's possible his wife, Monica, will take the helm. Although, my bet is she'll sell the business. She never had any interest in it, and her children are still in their teens. There's no one old enough to step into Dad's shoes yet. Nevertheless, the Sunridge Community is in full swing. I was told by Evan, the site manager, that contracts will be fulfilled. The company would lose far too much money to back out now. Even if Monica Madison wants to sell the company, I'm sure she'll want to finish this project. It's worth a lot of money, and there would be far too many legal troubles if they stopped."

"I read something about those too. Another community is suing because of all the problems they're having with their houses." I'd stepped on her tail again. Darn, and I'd been doing so well. We were almost chummy for a second.

She crinkled up her face. "The problems have been overblown. One woman is responsible for the uproar. You can't make a sound judgment based on those reviews. She has numerous people writing those. Some are not even Madison homeowners. Miss Blaine was dating Mr. Madison for a brief time. From what I understood, he tried to break it off congenially, but she took it badly. So, you see, her anger has nothing to do with her house. Besides, those homes are already three years old. Things are bound to go wrong once a house reaches three." She said it so confidently. It had to sound silly even to her ears.

"But this town is filled with houses that are two hundred plus years old. Surely, three is still a baby as far as houses are concerned. I have to say I'd hate to be dealing with big problems a mere three years after I bought the house."

Her bottom lip wrinkled up as if she'd sucked on a lemon. "Again, there are no big problems with Madison Homes. Only a scorned woman who decided to take her anger out on Rupert Madison."

The front door opened. A new, deer-in-the-headlights looking couple stepped in to see the model. They looked almost frightened about the prospect of buying a house. I couldn't blame them. It was a big deal, and, like me, everyone wanted to make the right choice. Barbara was quite pleased to have someone new to talk to. Her current potential homebuyer knew far too much and asked too many questions.

She straightened and plastered her saleswoman smile back on. "Take the brochure home with you and give it a look. I think you'll find Sunridge has a great deal to offer." With that, she motioned the way to the front door.

I smiled at the young couple and walked out. That was more productive than the visit to Lang Construction. So far, Veronica was holding the top spot on my suspect list. Barbara had mentioned Evan, the site manager. I wondered if he'd have anything interesting to add, not just about the murder but about Jeremy Sexton's firing. Couldn't be too hard to locate a site manager.

CHAPTER 23

In one section of the new development, hammers pounded almost rhythmically as five men framed a new house. The skeleton of the house was half-finished. Plumbers were working on the next property putting in the rough plumbing for bathrooms and kitchens. Two men were working with a forklift, removing pallets of brick pavers off the back of a truck.

"The realtor is inside the model," a voice said from behind. "You can't be out here without a hardhat and someone to guide you around. Barbara will give you a tour of the neighborhood." The man had a tough time keeping his hardhat straight on his bald head. His clothes were cleaner than most of the others, so I took a chance.

"Are you the site manager?"

He pushed the brim of his hardhat up to get a better look at me. "Speaking. I'm Evan."

It was time to use the press pass. I always preferred honest and straightforward. Since I was off my game today, it was the safest route. "I'm Sunni Taylor with the *Junction Times*. I was hoping you could answer a few questions about the man behind this development, Rupert Madison."

His expression hardened. "What do you want me to say?"

"Surely, you met and talked to him many times. I was hoping to talk to Curtis Lang too. Is he here?" I decided to toss the name out there to find out more information about the contractor.

"Why would Lang be out here? He started this project, but he didn't get along with Madison. He ended the contract. I was working for Lang, but Madison offered me a better job. He appointed me site manager. I coordinate the work and oversee the subcontractors."

"I see. I was here Tuesday morning. Madison gave me a tour of the neighborhood."

"I thought you looked familiar. Madison said something about a nosy reporter hanging around."

I smiled but it wasn't a gracious smile. "It's kind of our job to be nosy. There wouldn't be much to write about if we weren't."

"Well, I don't know anything about what happened," Evan said. "All I know is he was sitting at the outdoor movie, and someone shot him dead."

"Was there anyone in particular who might have had a grudge against the man?"

He chuckled. "You might say that. Not me though. I liked him. He gave me a lot of responsibility. Said he saw management potential in me. First time I've made good enough money to think about buying a house of my own."

"Would you buy a Madison home?" I asked.

He hesitated and seemed to be assessing why I asked the question. He nodded once. "You've been talking to Miss Blaine. Did she tell you Madison broke her heart? That's the only reason she's out there making such a fuss. She wants revenge. She's the one police need to question." I had to keep in mind that, like Barbara, Evan worked for Madison too. It seemed Rupert had filled everyone in on how he'd broken Veronica's heart and how that was the reason for her complaints. But I'd seen the other people in her HOA. They seemed genuinely disappointed with the quality of their homes.

"She's not the only person who has complaints about the quality of work on the Madison homes. I see this project is in full swing. I thought they might shut it down."

"Contracts are signed. People are waiting for their houses."

"Absolutely. The show must go on, as they say. Who do you think might take the helm at Madison's company?"

"Don't know anything about that. I'm just a site manager. I need to get back to work."

"One more question—about Jeremy Sexton—"

His eyes rounded. "How'd you know about Jeremy?"

"I was here when Madison fired him. It was cruelly done, and, frankly, I let Madison know how I felt."

Evan nodded slightly. "Jeremy was a good worker. He tried hard. Didn't mind doing some of the grunt work, like chopping up unused timber and picking up nails."

"So, you agree, he shouldn't have been fired over a tossed apple core?" I asked.

"Not my place to agree." Evan was still playing the part of the "yes man" even though his boss was dead.

"But you're site manager. Surely, you have a say over hiring and firing. Especially now—"

His attitude had softened. It seemed we had a mutual belief we'd coalesced around. We both knew Jeremy's firing was heavy-handed. "I left Jeremy a message this morning. Told him he could have his job back if he wanted it, but he hasn't called back."

"I imagine he was feeling pretty humiliated. I witnessed the whole exchange. I felt badly for him."

"Me too."

"Was Jeremy close to any of the other workers? I'd love to ask a few questions about Jeremy's reaction. I never spoke to him after he was dismissed."

"We're very busy out here." He glanced around and whistled. "Larry, can you come over here for a second?" Evan turned back to me. "Only a few minutes. Everyone is on the clock right now. Larry and Jeremy sometimes went out for beer after work."

A young man with a dark tan and a ship anchor tattooed on his forearm hurried over. "Yeah, boss?"

"This is Sunni Taylor with the *Junction Times*. She has a few questions about Jeremy." Evan walked away.

Larry looked at me skeptically. "Is he all right?"

"I'm sure he's fine. I was here when Jeremy got fired. I think I saw you at the lunch table."

"That's right. You were with Madison when Jeremy pitched that apple core. That was some really bad luck."

"It was. I let Madison know that I thought firing Jeremy was harsh."

"Yeah, Mad Madison, that's what we used to call him." He dropped his face. "Not anymore, of course."

"Of course. Did you talk to Jeremy afterward?"

"Yeah, he came by after he picked up his gear. He was spitting mad. He'd finally found a good job. That's what he told me. He and his girlfriend were going to find a nice place together. He had all kinds of plans. Evan is going to hire him back now that—well—now that Madison is gone."

"Do you think he'll come back?"

"I don't see why not. I tried to call him this morning, but he wasn't answering his phone. He'll be back. I'm sure of it."

"Larry, we need you," someone called from the house being framed.

"I'll let you go. One last thing—have the police come to the site to talk to you guys?"

He looked surprised by the question. "Not that I know of."

"I thought maybe since—"

"It's true then. No one is really talking about it, but we're hearing it was murder."

"I'm afraid so."

Larry seemed to decide he shouldn't have said so much about Jeremy. "Jeremy would never do it. He was mad about getting fired." Larry smiled. "He texted me after he soaked Madison in the dunk tank. He even took a picture." Larry reached into the back pocket of his pants and pulled out his phone. His callused thumb scrolled over the screen, then he held it up for me. It was a photo of a dripping wet Rupert Madison standing in the dunk tank. He was scowling angrily through the Plexiglass. Interestingly enough, Jeremy's own reflection was caught on it too. He glared right back at the man in the tank. I'd been there to witness the dunking, but I hadn't noticed the silent, angry exchange between the two men.

"Looks like Jeremy got his revenge," I said as I handed him back the phone. "Thanks for your time."

Larry nodded and took off back toward the hammering.

I headed back to the Jeep. My phone buzzed with a text as I climbed inside. It was Jackson. I held my breath as I opened the text. I wasn't sure what to expect.

"Want to have a cup of coffee? At the coffee shop. Somewhere we can talk without a third party listening in."

My finger was shaky as I wrote back. Was this it? Was Jackson going to break up with me? I should have been happy he wanted to have coffee, but my limbs were feeling as if they'd been filled with lead. I had a bad feeling about the cup of coffee. I needed to prepare myself for the worst and hope for the best.

"Sure, I'll see you there in fifteen." I sent off the text and released the breath I'd been holding.

CHAPTER 24

I was a teenager again, belly full of jittery of butterflies as I waited for a first date. Only this was far from a first date. Would it be the last? I'd told myself to prepare for the worst. If Jackson decided he could no longer be with me because I came with some *baggage*, then I'd learn how to move on. The words sounded stoic and full of resolve in my head, but my heart was giving me a whole different scenario. Losing Jackson would be utterly and wholly devastating. It would take me a long time to recover. And living in the same town would make it impossible to forget him, let alone suffer the misery of seeing him with someone else.

I was practically sick with worry by the time I pulled into the parking lot. Jackson's work car was parked outside the coffee shop. He'd seen me pull up and texted. "I already bought you a mocha latte."

"Thanks," I texted back. It all sounded so dry and unromantic. Usually our texts were flirty. Not today. Today we were in a "we need to talk" mode. No fun or flirting involved.

I glanced up and checked my face. I'd only slashed on a touch of mascara this morning. I thought I was headed out for some reporting and investigation. I hadn't expected coffee with Jackson to be part of my day.

I opened the door to the shop. Van Morrison music poured down from the speakers, and the rich aroma of coffee swirled around my head. I could think of worse places to have my heart stepped on and demolished. Jackson was always easy to spot in any room, even if it was crowded. It was past peak coffee time, so only a few tables were occupied.

Jackson had grabbed our favorite table in the back nook. My mocha latte sat across from him. His amber gaze followed me to the table.

"Hey," he said quietly.

"Hey." I sat down and took hold of the coffee. It was more of a security blanket at this point. I didn't even feel like coffee. It would only make me more anxious, and I didn't need that today. At least I had a few things other than *us* to talk about. "I saw Detective Willow leaving the pharmacy this morning."

"Yep, he pulled his back. He insists he'll be back in a few days, but I'm not so sure."

"Me neither," I said. "He was moving like a sloth when I saw him. Took him an eternity just to get into his car."

Jackson let go of his coffee and sat back. "Have you been conducting your usual shadow investigation alongside mine?"

"Yes, and I prefer to think of it as a complementary investigation rather than a shadow one. How is yours going?"

"Now that I got sidetracked with the case Willow's been working on, a homicide in Smithville, I'm not doing great. I'm focused on Veronica Blaine. She seemed to have a list of possible motives."

"And—as I understand it—she's quite handy with a gun."

Jackson tried hard not to look impressed, but he couldn't help himself. "You've been doing your research. The person who shot Madison had to know how to handle a gun."

"As long as Rupert was the target and not some random victim," I noted.

"This seemed planned."

"Have you talked to Curtis Lang?" I asked. "I drove out to his construction office in Birch Highlands today. That's when I spotted Roy coming out of the pharmacy."

Jackson pulled his notebook out and flipped through it. We were sitting, having coffee and chatting as if everything was fine. Was the bad part of the visit waiting to rear its ugly head and send me off crying? I doubted Jackson would have a lengthy conversation about the case if he had that particular bomb to drop. He pulled out a pen and wrote down the name.

"Lang Construction, right?" Jackson asked.

"Yes, the owner is Curtis."

"Yeah, I know him. He's built a few things in the area."

"He built a neighborhood for Madison. Veronica's neighborhood, in fact. If everything she says is true, Curtis followed Madison's lead in cutting corners and letting inspectors look the other way. He started as the contractor of Madison's latest project, Sunridge Community, but according to the site manager, Lang wasn't getting along with Rupert, so they parted ways. Nevertheless, Lang decided to put in a bid to build Madison's shopping center. From what I've heard, that didn't pan out either."

Jackson wrote down a few notes. "Guess the complementary investigation is going a lot better than the real one."

"Especially now that you've got to split your time."

Jackson put away his notebook. "Wasn't expecting that glitch. Not to mention, my head is not really into it this week." He looked at me over our cups of coffee. "Bluebird, I'm sorry I've been so grumpy. It's just—I'm usually pretty good at problem solving, but this is way bigger and more impossible, not to mention, weirder, than any problem I've ever faced."

"You don't have to tell me that. As much as I was relieved to be able to share my secret with you, I sometimes think it would be easier if I was the only person who could see and hear Edward."

"That would almost be creepier. At least, now I know that he exists." He got quiet. His dark lashes covered his eyes as he fidgeted with his coffee cup. His shoulders lifted and fell. "At the risk of sounding like a spoiled kid, it'd be nice if you sided with me sometimes whenever Gramps—I mean, Edward and I get into it."

"I do side with you. Don't I? Actually, I guess I usually scold both of you, but that's because sometimes it feels like I'm stuck inside a really bad case of sibling rivalry."

Jackson sat back again. "It's a rivalry, but not the kind you think. I've told you before—Edward is in love with you. He's in a competition. I'm competing for the girl I love with a man who literally only exists in spirit. It seems like it should be easier than an actual flesh and blood man but it's not. He's everywhere. He's always there."

"There's an easy way to solve that," I said. "We can spend more time at your place."

"You've got the cool house," he reminded me.

"That I do."

"And we're planning our future at Cider Ridge with the barn and animals." He paused and looked at me. "Maybe we should put those plans on hold."

It was the first truly heartbreaking thing he'd said. "I've already put my inn idea on the backburner. I can't allow Edward to change my future again. At the same time—I feel a great deal of empathy when it comes to him. He's stuck in that house for eternity. When I put myself in his shoes, well, his boots—it would be such a long prison sentence. He was alone in that house, drifting through the empty, cold hallways for years. And, as you've noticed, he loves to socialize. He enjoys talking to us."

Jackson rested back and blew out a puff of air. "I know. Can't be easy for him. Honestly, I like talking to him sometimes. He knows a lot about horses. It's cool to see how different his views from centuries ago are. At the same time, he's exhausting. And privacy is scarce in that house."

I was so relieved we weren't talking about a breakup that I'd let go some of the anxiety and regained my confidence. I leaned forward and reached across for his hand. I held it between mine. "All I know is I want to spend the rest of my life with you, Jax. I don't have any plans to sell Cider Ridge. I love the place, and I put in so much time and money—there's no way I could sell it to some strangers. It's a part of me, and I've got my sisters close by."

He covered my hand with his free hand. "I'd never ask you to do that. I love the place too, and I want to spend the rest of my life with you. I was thinking, however, that I'd keep my humble little Grizzly Adams style cabin for when we need more privacy or when I've had a bad day and I can't deal with our *elephant*."

I laughed. "Poor guy. It took him awhile to figure out that we were talking about him and not an actual elephant."

Jackson laughed. "It is fun teasing him with modern day lingo."

"It is, and I don't mind it as long as you two can keep it to a minimum. Sometimes, things get out-of-hand. Especially when I'm in the room, and about that—"

"That's because when you're in the room, Edward is trying to out alpha male me. Like I said—he loves you. He considers me a rival, even though he knows nothing can come of it. It's another reason I sometimes feel sorry for the guy." He lifted my hand and gazed at me as he kissed the back of it. "I can't imagine how hard it would be to be madly in love with Sunni Taylor and know I could never have her."

Tears welled up in my eyes. "I was worried you were going to leave me."

"Not in a million years, Bluebird."

CHAPTER 25

I pulled up to the house, my fabulous, stylish, old gem with its hidden secret between the walls, and allowed myself a short sob session. Jackson and I spent the rest of our coffee date talking about the barn and the future farm. He had plans to start a large vegetable plot. I teased him that he was coming up with every reason he could think of to rent the big tractor. He had a blast driving that thing around the property. He didn't disagree. He walked me to the car and bestowed upon me a kiss that would rival that of any fairytale prince.

Raine texted me before I got out of the Jeep. "Are we still making salad at your place?"

During my afternoon on an emotional rollercoaster, I'd forgotten that Raine and I had made plans for a late summer dinner. My mood was so much better, I looked forward to it. "Absolutely. See you soon," I texted back.

She sent another text. "Sounds like your mood is better. I've been getting good vibes all afternoon."

"Your sixth sense is right again. I'll tell you about it over salad."

Edward slipped through the wall and met me on the front stoop. "I'll lock myself up. No one uses the upstairs bedroom. I can stay in there, and you'll never have to see me again."

"Afternoon to you too," I said.

"I'm quite resolved to stay in that room for the rest of my— well, for eternity. I don't want to be an elephant anymore. I understand I'm a nuisance. Brady and you have every right to live your lives in the house. If I could figure a way out of this place, I'd go."

He looked so genuinely sad that I wished I could hug him. "Edward, you don't need to lock yourself away. You have a small enough world as it is. Besides, I'd miss talking to you."

His blue eyes scrutinized my face. "Are you being sincere?"

"Of course. The Cider Ridge is your home too. I would never confine you to one space."

His image shuddered. It seemed to be from relief. "What about Brady?"

"What about him? It'll be his home too. I would like to ask one big favor though."

"Yes?"

"Can you cool it on the constant insults? And that includes talking about his wild hair. Men these days do not tie their long hair back in ribbons like they did in your century."

He looked confused. "I don't understand. What am I cooling?"

"Bad choice of words." The dogs heard me out on the stoop. Redford's big, smiling face appeared in the front window. His tail wagged wildly behind him. I unlocked the door. Edward followed me inside. He waited for the exuberant dog greeting to end. I patted and hugged both dogs, then they tore off toward the kitchen and their treat (the real motive behind the big, showy greeting).

I put my things down and pulled the treat jar out of the

pantry. Each dog took their cookie and trotted off to their personal pillow to enjoy the snack in plush comfort.

I pulled the romaine lettuce and bag of baby spinach out of the refrigerator to chop. Edward waited patiently for me to explain myself. Although, I thought, even with using the modern slang *cool* it was self-explanatory.

I tossed the greens into the colander and turned on the faucet. "I need you to stop agitating Jackson. I've asked him to tone it down too. The two of you need to get along. Otherwise, my head will explode. Not literally, of course."

"Of course. I'm not an imbecile."

"Right. Well, for a brief time, you thought we were having a problem with elephants."

"Not true. I didn't grasp your meaning because you are constantly talking about the most nonsensical things."

"Thank you for that." I turned off the water. "See, you're very opinionated, and sometimes, you should just keep those opinions to yourself."

"I hardly see how that would help. My opinions are valuable."

I lifted the colander, gave it a shake to remove excess water and tossed the greens onto my cutting board. "They aren't as valuable as you imagine."

He paused to reflect on that possibility. I knew him well enough that I could predict exactly what would come from his moment of quiet contemplation.

"No, that can't be right." (Yes, that was what I'd predicted.)

I spun around to face him. "Then, how about this—when you feel one of those priceless opinions welling up inside of you, float upstairs, lock yourself in the room and voice it."

"Then no one will hear or benefit from the opinion," he said.

"Exactly." I turned back to the greens.

"Oh dear, it's the daft woman with the armful of bracelets, colorful skirts and inane conversation."

I stopped chopping and inadvertently pointed at him with the knife I was holding. He stared down at it with apprehension.

"Oops, sorry." I put the knife down.

"It's not as if you can stab me," he noted.

I rolled my eyes. "Anyhow, that long-winded opinion you just shared—that would be far more valuable if you went upstairs and said it to yourself. Or even better, kept it entirely in your head."

"None of that makes sense to me. Then strikingly good opinions would be entirely wasted."

"And that is *your* opinion," I said with a smile before heading to the door behind the dogs. They knew Raine would have a pocketful of treats.

Raine handed me a basket with tomatoes and cucumbers from her garden. "Does Auntie Raine have cookies?" She paused dramatically. Both dogs waited with bated breath as she made a show of fishing around in the big pockets on her skirt. "Ah ha," she cheered as she held up two dog treats. "Here you go, my handsome devils." She handed them each a treat. They ran back to their pillows as if that was their first treat of the day.

Edward appeared in the entryway.

"Edward," Raine said happily. She pushed a stray strand of hair off her face. "You're here." She hadn't expected him at the door and was a little tongue-tied.

"Where else would I be?" he drawled.

I shot him a "be nice" scowl. After the lengthy talk with my ghost, I realized it was all for naught. Nothing ever penetrated his highly penetrable head.

"It's just that you seem to avoid making yourself visible when I'm around."

"It seems that way, does it?" he asked wryly. I scowled again.

He turned back to Raine. "You're imaging that, of course. I always look forward very much to seeing you. I stand in that window morning and night wondering when I might see you again." He looked at me for approval.

"A little thick," I noted.

"He's being sarcastic, right?" Raine asked.

"You know how cars have a neutral gear?" I asked as I headed toward the kitchen with the basket of vegetables. Raine followed. Edward was already in the kitchen as I arrived. "Sarcasm and acerbic wit are Edward's neutral gear. Anything else, like politeness"—I looked at him pointedly—"takes a movement of gears."

"I don't understand. What is this neutral gear you speak of?" he asked.

I waved him away. "Go do something else. Raine and I are going to have dinner." He actually listened, a rarity. But he also hated hanging around too long when Raine was over.

We got to work making our delicious salads. The salad had been Raine's idea. She said she hadn't eaten enough vegetables in a few weeks and was starting to feel ashamed about it. I hadn't gone heavy enough on the greens either lately, so I readily fell in line with her guilt trip.

"How's it going? My senses tell me the trouble in paradise was short-lived." Raine put a freshly washed tomato on the cutting board.

"Your senses are right." I took a deep breath. "I was so scared, Raine. And then I scared myself more when I realized how devastating it would be to lose Jackson. So much for being a strong, independent woman."

"Nonsense. You can be strong, independent and hopelessly in love."

I looked at her. "You're right, Raine. I am all three of those things. Of course, the hopelessly in love part is the only one that relies on Jackson. But I think we're past this latest hurdle. We have something good. It'd be crazy to let one pompous ghost ruin that."

"I'm not pompous," he said from somewhere in the room.

"You are the very definition of pompous," I called back.

"See, that's always a little creepy when his disembodied voice comes out of nowhere," Raine said.

Edward appeared. "I thought you were a soothsayer. You must hear disembodied voices all the time."

Raine looked at me. "Neutral gear, right?"

"Yep. It's his go-to gear. I'll get the bowls. These salads are going to be delicious, and, at least for today, we'll have satisfied the nutritional gods."

CHAPTER 26

A frantic knock on the front door made me choke on my coffee. I coughed all the way to the door and finally gathered myself together as I opened it. Lauren was pacing a small circle on the front stoop. She was wearing a yellow sundress, and her makeup looked a little messy. I'd never seen her with messy makeup.

"Lauren, what's wrong? Come inside. My sister made me some blueberry muffins."

"I didn't want to bother you so early, but you're the only person who'll understand my problem."

Her sandals clicked delicately in the hallway as we headed to the kitchen. It took a special talent and an exceptionally graceful gait to walk quietly in sandals, but Lauren managed it. Lauren had come to the house twice for lunch, and Edward always found her, as he put it, one of my more "delightful acquaintances."

He was already perched on the hearth waiting for us as we entered the kitchen. "Finally, an agreeable guest," he muttered. He knew he was going to be engaged in an entirely one-sided conversation during Lauren's visit. I'd grown quite skilled at ignoring him when I had non-informed visitors in the house. It was a skill I wished I could teach to Jackson, so he could ignore Edward, not just with visitors but all the time.

I placed a muffin on a plate and poured Lauren a cup of coffee. "Do you have any almond milk?" she asked. "Never mind. I'll drink it black."

"Since when do almonds provide us with milk?" Edward asked. "Absurd. What's next? Sugar from corn?"

I pulled in my lip to avoid smiling and sat next to Lauren. "Now, tell me, what has you so upset?"

"I have writer's block," she said it in a whisper as if it was a contagious malady.

"Oh, that." I laughed lightly. "It'll pass."

She was shaking her head. "Not this time. I had so many good notes and cute little anecdotes about the end-of-summer fair. The corn dog eating contest was hysterical. All the contestants had mustard smeared from ear to ear. Anyhow, I can't pull together any article because—" She picked a piece off the muffin but didn't eat it. "Because I don't know how to write about murder. I write about fashion and travel trends and pet adoption events, but I've never had to write about anything as sad as death."

"I hadn't considered that, Lauren. I can see where you might feel hesitant. However, true journalism covers both the good and the bad. Pet adoptions make for a fun, uplifting read. However, an article about the murder of a prominent local businessman is intriguing and informative. People want to know what's happening in their neighborhood. That's why those neighborhood apps are so popular. Occasionally, people post things like new puppies or farm fresh produce for sale. Sometimes, they post about their car being broken into or their cat missing. It's the good and the bad. Just keep to the facts. You don't need to provide gory details."

Lauren's lip turned up. She wasn't convinced. "I don't think I can do that. Last night, I started the article five times and deleted everything I wrote each time." Her normally perky posture deflated. "Aunt Prudence is counting on me to deliver something *noteworthy and captivating*. I can show you the text. Those were her exact words."

"It appears not everyone is enthralled with murder like you," Edward mused. He'd moved to the table area, *enthralled* with my visitor. I was sure it had mostly to do with her youth and beauty. Edward had carried his shallowness through to death and beyond. I couldn't blame him. Lauren had that special something that made her extra likable. And I felt bad about her predicament. At the same time, if she wanted to be a journalist, she was going to have to take the good, the bad and the ugly into consideration. It was a package deal in journalism.

Lauren finally ate the small piece of muffin. Her eyebrows danced happily. "Your sister, Emily, is so talented. Everything she bakes is like magic. Best blueberry muffin I've ever had." She pulled out her phone. "I'm going to message her about it."

"She'll be pleased."

She sent off a quick message and smiled. "See, I feel better. I'm more of a positive energy person. Like your sister. I should tell Prue to give you the murder story."

"I guess I'm the negative, murder-y side of the family," I quipped.

"You do have an affinity for it," Edward noted. He was energetic this morning, mostly because of the visitor. Plus, he enjoyed when all the comments were coming from one direction, namely his. I was having to bite my tongue a lot.

Lauren laughed. "Of course, you're not the murder-y sister. It's just—" Her cute, perfectly plucked brows bunched. "It's just —you do seem to run into a lot of—a lot of—"

"Dead people?" I asked.

She bit her lip. "Sorry, that was in poor taste. I don't know what's wrong with me. I'm not usually so socially clumsy. I'm blaming it on this assignment. What should I do, Sunni? I need to hear your advice, no matter how brutal. Go on. Give it to me. I can take it."

Looking at her young, innocent face I found that hard to believe, but she asked for my advice. I was, after all, supposed to be her mentor. She hadn't learned journalism in college where the professors handed out torturously dull or excessively brutal topics to get you to stretch your abilities. Those were the kinds of assignments that let you step out of the box. They let you test the water and test your own limits. Lauren's entire education had been from writing spunky, charming posts online. The fact that she usually delivered them in front of a camera helped gain her followers. She was engaging and pretty and stylish, all the things that people, my ghost included, found captivating.

"I'm going to give it you straight, Lauren. All right?"

"Absolutely." She shifted on her seat, straightened her posture and gave me her all ears look. Only her "all ears" look reminded me of a cute bunny waiting to be fed a carrot. I lost my nerve.

"Don't leave the girl waiting," Edward prodded.

"Lauren, I know you and you don't just hate to fail. You loathe it. If you don't write this, you'll be disappointed in yourself. You can't turn down a story because it has a dark or unpleasant element. I guess what I'm saying is—you can keep writing the wonderful, sugary stories for the paper, or you can get your feet a little dirty. Step into the mud. I think you might find it interesting. Controversy, crime, deception all make for great articles. They're the kinds of things that keep people reading the paper."

She sat still for a second. I worried she might cry. Instead, she threw her arms up and gave me a hug. "I knew you were the right person to talk to. I woke up this morning in such a state I could hardly drag a mascara brush through my lashes. I mean, look at me. I'm half clown today. But I said to myself, 'Lauren, you need to head over to that beautiful Cider Ridge and talk to your mentor and the world's smartest journalist, Sunni Taylor.'"

Edward scoffed. "She might be a little frillier in the head than I first thought."

I glared at him. Lauren was so astute, she glanced back. "Who are you looking at? You look mad about something. Are you mad at me?" she asked frantically. Lauren was definitely someone who wasn't used to being scowled at.

"No, of course not." I pressed my hand against my stomach and repeated my scowl. "It's just this annoying bout of indigestion I keep getting. Can't seem to get rid of it," I said with a pointed glance at Edward.

Lauren's mouth turned down. "You should have a doctor check that out. My aunt once thought she had indigestion. It turned out she was pregnant."

"She really does have a head filled with lace and cotton. Pity. She seemed so clever." Edward vanished.

"I'm sure it's the coffee. Are you going to write the story? You can always send me your drafts, and I can give you pointers."

"Would you? You're the best." She hugged me again. "I guess I'd better get to the office and start writing. Are you going to be in the newsroom?"

"Possibly but I've got a few places to stop first." I'd woken with a solid plan in my head to get to the bottom of the Madison murder. "I might even have some information to add to your article by the time I'm back."

She clapped a few times fast. "Perfect. Now, I'm looking forward to the assignment because I'll be working closely with my amazing mentor."

CHAPTER 27

I'd accomplished at least one good deed for the day, and it was still early. If I could solve the murder, it would make my day stunningly complete. Life always seemed to go like that. I'd been worried and fretting for a few days. Suddenly, the sunlight turned back on, and I was smiling and humming a tune. And I hummed that tune ("Jingle Bells," for some odd reason, considering the season) all the way to Robert Higgins' farm.

It occurred to me, as I sorted out the suspects over my cup of coffee, that Mr. Higgins had possibly the most to gain from Rupert's death. In the interim, while the higher-ups at the Madison Company figured out what to do without their top man, the shopping center would certainly be on hold. It was even possible they'd drop the idea altogether. It was a risky venture and would cost the company a great deal of capital. Profits were not guaranteed. It seemed the shopping center was more of a vanity project for Rupert. It was another chance to display his wealth and power by showcasing a shopping center with his name on it.

The sun was already way hotter than I would have liked as I parked and got out of the Jeep in front of the farm. Summer was clinging to its last throes of power before autumn swept in like a refreshing breeze to cool down the temperature, dry up the humidity and tell the billions of flying insects to take a break.

Robert Higgins was wearing a white t-shirt, jeans and a wide-brimmed straw hat as he stood in his chicken yard doling out scratch. The chickens kicked up a sizable dust storm as they circled around him like a tornado of feathers, scurrying to get their share of the feed. His cattle were sitting in the pasture under various trees, settled down for a few hours of digestion and chewing cud.

I headed up the dirt driveway. Higgins held the brim of his hat and lifted his face. "Can I help you?" he asked.

I waved my pass. "It's me, Sunni Taylor."

"I'll be right there." The chickens clucked a loud, throaty chorus as Higgins finished tossing out the cracked corn. "That's enough for now, ladies," he chortled as he stepped out of the coop. He looked to be in a much better mood than the last time we spoke. I was too, for that matter.

Higgins pulled a rag from his back pocket and wiped off his hands. "How can I help you, Miss Taylor?"

"I hoped to get a few comments from you about the latest turn in events." I'd submitted my story early, not really having much appetite for writing it, but it had grown more intriguing with Madison's death. I sent Prudence an email telling her to disregard my first draft entirely because there would be more to add. She, of course, wrote back "I should think so." Like Edward, she had an ability to make every sentence, even in email, sound condescending.

"Right. I guess things have taken a rather interesting turn, haven't they?" He wasn't rejoicing, but he wasn't exactly glum. "I made a fresh batch of sun tea. Care for some over ice? I've got fresh lemons too."

"That sounds perfect." I followed him to the farmhouse. He had a slight limp and took the steps slowly.

The inside was quaint and cozy, except for the thin layer of dust on everything. The furniture, the old sofa and chairs sitting around a red and green braided rug, looked heavily used and comfy. An antique-looking rifle was mounted above the wood mantel on a brick fireplace. A fat, gray cat looked up from the front windowsill as we headed into the kitchen.

The sink had a pile of dishes. The faint smell of bacon wafted up from the stove. I sat at the small table and waited as he poured us each a glass of tea topped with a lemon slice.

"That's an interesting rifle hanging over the mantel." The gun caught my eye immediately. The police had the murder weapon, but it seemed to me to shoot someone dead in the middle of a crowd you had to be able to shoot like the Sundance Kid. At the very least, you had to be skilled with a gun.

"Isn't that something?" he said with pride. "It's an 1861 Springfield, used in the Civil War." He returned to the table with the teas and sat down across from me. "I'm a collector."

"Of Civil War relics or guns?" I asked.

"Both."

We took a sip of tea.

"Hmm, tart and tasty," I noted.

"I think this might be my best batch yet."

"Are you able to still use that gun?"

"Not that one. She's too valuable. The patina on the butt and barrel, you don't find that on a new rifle. That gun has seen things. She's experienced battle, death and triumph. I have hunting rifles, but they don't have that kind of history. I used to be an avid hunter, but my knees have taken me out of the game."

He reached down and rubbed his right knee. "Doc says I need a new one, but I went online to research what they do and no thank you. I'll stick with my limp. The pain's not too bad in the summer. Kicks in more in winter."

"That makes sense. I have some old sports injuries, an overused shoulder and a bad ankle. I forget about them all year until the weather turns cold. Then I have to drag out the heating pads."

He was nodding along. "Yep, those heating pads are great. Except they only take away the pain when they're on ya. Once you turn them off and walk away, it comes right back. I'm still able to take care of the farm. Once I can't do that anymore, I'll think about that new knee."

"But you won't need to worry about the farm soon. I didn't see a sign yet."

"Nope and you won't. I'm not going anywhere."

I sat up straighter. "You're not going to sell?"

"No need to." He took a sip of tea and sighed at the refreshing goodness. "It's these new tea bags. They have a hint of lemon in them. There's no reason for me to sell anymore."

"I don't understand. Have they already decided not to build the shopping center?" Had Higgins jumped to that conclusion based on the sole fact that Madison was dead?

"I probably shouldn't say anything because it's not public knowledge yet, but Jim Ortho, my lawyer, happens to be in the firm that is handling Madison's estate. Everything was left to Monica Madison, the wife. Jim called me this morning to say Monica had already been in touch with the law firm. She has no interest in running the Madison Company. She's planning to sell the whole kit and caboodle. She wants to open a string of yoga studios with the money. Sounded a little crazy to me, but I don't care if she opens up doggie hair salons just as long as that darn shopping center is never built."

"But if she sells the company, won't the new owners continue with those plans?" I asked.

"No guarantee, and Jim said we could start the litigation all over again. It could be years before they even break ground."

The gray cat had grown bored of watching the front yard birds. He meowed quietly as he walked into the kitchen and rubbed against my leg. I leaned down to pet him. "What about your grandkids?"

"I'll still see 'em plenty. They love to spend time out here at the farm. I feel awful that Madison died, but I won't lie, this has turned my life right side up again. I wasn't being honest with myself before. I'm not ready to retire and give up the farm. Still got a few good years kicking around in me."

"I don't blame you. It'd be hard to give up a lifestyle you're so used to." I finished the tea and stood with the empty glass.

Higgins took the glass and added it to the pile in the sink. "I've got chores to do. Thanks for stopping by. And remember, don't mention anything my lawyer told me. It'll be common knowledge soon enough." We stepped out onto the front porch. Some of the chickens had migrated out into the yard to look for bugs.

"I'm glad this turned out well for you, Mr. Higgins." I turned back to him and tossed out one more casual question. "I know you were at the summer fair. Did you stick around for movie night?"

"Nah, I have to get up too early to stay out late like that. I was fast asleep in bed, in case you were wondering whether or not I killed Madison."

I startled a little at his frankness. "Wouldn't be a journalist if I didn't ask the important questions. Have a good day." I headed down the dirt driveway to the Jeep. Higgins was one person who'd gained a lot from Madison's death. He had a flimsy alibi, and he knew how to use a gun. He didn't act the least bit cagey and invited me right in for a chat. Would a killer do that? Maybe. Seemed I had a new person at the top of my list.

CHAPTER 28

To top off my so far productive, pleasant day, as I left the Higgins farm, Emily texted that she needed a lunchtime taste tester for a new egg salad recipe. I texted Jackson that I had some information about the case, but I hadn't heard back from him. Poor guy was busy on two cases. It felt nice to be able to text him after our few days without communication.

I spotted Emily's pale pink t-shirt in the chicken coop as I pulled up to her farm. A customer was standing outside the coop with a basket of fresh eggs. The woman looked familiar, mostly because of the teased orange hair. It was Felicity Rossdale, the woman who unwittingly sold her husband's gun for the price of a used suitcase.

Emily carried out a few more eggs. "Hey, sis," she called from under the brim of her hat.

Felicity turned back to see who Emily was greeting. A flicker of recognition crossed her face. "Is this your sister, Emily?" Her rust brown eyebrows bunched together. "Where have I met you?" she asked me.

"I was at your house with Detective Jackson."

"That's right," she said it with enough enthusiasm that the eggs rolled around the basket. "Oops, don't want to break these."

Emily added a few more to the basket. "There we go. That's a dozen. Do you have any big plans for the eggs?" Emily started the walk to her small shed where she kept a cash box and her credit card reader.

"Boris's birthday is Sunday, so I'll bake him his favorite vanilla-caramel cake." She handed Emily a twenty-dollar bill.

"Hmm, that sounds good." Emily stepped into the shed to get Felicity's change.

Felicity turned to me. She was wearing bright lipstick to go with her hair. Her cheeks and forehead were pink from the sun. "I left a message for Detective Jackson, but I haven't heard back from him."

I perked forward with full attention. "Did you remember who you sold the suitcase to?" That suitcase and its hidden contents could likely solve the case.

"Well, not entirely. But I do remember it was a young woman. Brown hair, I think."

"A young woman with brown hair," I repeated. That narrowed it down to about five thousand people in town.

Emily returned and handed off the change. "Is this about the Madison murder?"

"Yes, can you believe that ridiculous husband of mine? Apparently, on his brother Morty's advice"—she rolled her eyes —"he bought a gun for protection. But he was so uncomfortable with it in the house, he hid it in an old suitcase and then stuck the suitcase in the garage rafters. I said to him this morning, after the stupidity of it all became clearer to me, 'Boris, how were you going to protect us from a robbery? Were you going to ask the thief to sit still while you went out to the garage, grabbed the stepladder, climbed up to the rafters, carried down the suitcase and opened it?' Not exactly a brilliant security plan."

Emily and I couldn't hide our amusement.

Felicity joined us with a laugh. "I mean have you ever heard of anything so harebrained?"

"I suppose it would be hard to fend off an intruder if your gun was in the garage rafters," I said. "Can you think of anything else about the woman who bought the suitcase? Did she happen to give her name?"

"No, and I was only accepting cash that day. My card reader wasn't working. I didn't get a name, but she said she was going on a spiritual retreat next month, so she needed a new suitcase. She was wearing big sunglasses, so I didn't get a good look at her face. I assume she lives nearby because she came on a bicycle. She was worried about getting the suitcase home on the bike. I suggested she could leave it and come back later with a car, but she insisted she could ride slowly with one hand holding the suitcase."

"Have you ever seen her before?" I asked.

"I don't think so. Like I said, she was wearing big sunglasses." She snapped her fingers as something occurred to her. "I do remember one detail that made her stand out from the flurry of customers at the yard sale. She was wearing a big pink crystal around her neck. It dangled from a long gold chain. She rubbed it a few times while she was looking around. I noticed it because it was quite large and a beautiful shade of pink. I told her it reminded me of pink lemonade. She said she wore it because it helped her energy stay positive."

I looked at Emily. She smiled back. "Raine will know her."

"Exactly."

Felicity looked back and forth between us. "Did that help? I still can't believe that gun was used to kill someone. Just horrifying. I can assure you Boris is now searching the internet for big dogs. No more guns in our house."

"Dogs are a good, loud deterrent, and they're lovable too," Emily noted.

"Absolutely. Boris has always wanted one. He's very excited. I better get these eggs out of the hot sun. Otherwise, they'll be hard-boiled."

"Thanks for your help, Felicity. I think I know how to find the woman who bought the suitcase."

Felicity grimaced. "Was she the killer? I hadn't considered that. Maybe she lost track of that pink crystal and all her positive energy." She waved. "See you next week, Emily."

Emily took off her hat and fluffed her hair with her fingers. "I'm officially tired of the heat. Ready for lunch?"

"I am. And I agree. We've had more than our share of summer this year. I'm looking forward to fall."

Emily pointed toward her large pumpkin patch. "Starting to see little green pumpkins, always a sure sign that fall is coming." We climbed the back steps. Emily reached up and rang the cowbell hanging by the back door to summon Nick to lunch. "I highly recommend one of these bells when the farm starts up. I can't believe how long I went without one. Nick doesn't like to take his phone out to the barn. He's dropped it in more than one pile of soft manure. Not a pretty sight. I was having to walk around the whole farm to find him for mealtime, and everything was cold by the time I rounded him up." She motioned across the barnyard. Nick was walking out of the barn. He waved at me and I waved back. "See, I've got him trained like one of Pavlov's dogs. He hears the bell and comes running."

I laughed as we stepped into the kitchen. Emily crinkled her nose. "I love egg salad, but making it always leaves me with a stinky kitchen. I'm going to write a new blog post about dealing with stinky stuff like broccoli, cauliflower"—she turned from the refrigerator with a tray of egg salad sandwiches—"and hard-boiled eggs." She placed them on the table. "I've got a jar of homemade pickles too if you're interested."

"When am I not interested in homemade pickles?"

"Me, too," Nick said as he entered the kitchen. "How's it going, Sunni? You and Farmer Jackson track down Rupert Madison's killer yet?"

"Not yet, but I just had a productive conversation with one of your egg customers that I think will get me closer to the golden egg."

CHAPTER 29

After stuffing myself silly with Emily's delicious egg salad (I gave her two thumbs up on the taste test) I headed home to check on the dogs and the goats. The mighty star above had turned up the thermostat another few degrees. Every inch of me stuck to the seats in the Jeep as I made the short trip home from Emily's farm.

I stepped inside. My house had this magical way of staying cool without the expense of air conditioning. It was surrounded by trees, and the walls were thick and sturdy. That said, it also had a non-magical way of staying cold in the winter no matter how high I turned the thermostat. Today, the magic was working in the right direction. I felt instantly refreshed standing in the entryway. Edward didn't see it that way.

"Why on earth do you look like that?" he asked.

"Oh, Edward, you and your confidence building ways."

My phone rang. It was Jackson. The dogs trotted down the hall to meet me with far less enthusiasm and timing than usual. Unlike humans, they had no way to take off their thick coats. "Hot enough for ya?" I asked as I answered the phone.

"No kidding. I ordered a chocolate shake to go with my burger, and it was milk and chocolate syrup by the time I got it back to the station."

"But you drank it anyway," I said.

"Well, yeah, it was milk and chocolate syrup. I hope you're doing better than me on this case. I was in Smithville all morning working on Willow's case. Finally got a confession out of a very perturbed fast-food manager. Let's just say, the french fries gave it away."

"Sounds like Smithville's murders are more fun than ours. I'll have to hear about that one."

"You may never eat fries again."

"Then never mind. I prefer to keep my love affair with French fries intact."

"What have you got?"

"I drove out to the Higgins Farm to see Robert Higgins. It seems he is no longer selling his farm. He told me this in confidence but then he didn't know I had the ear of the police on speed dial. The lawyer he used for the lawsuit trying to stop Madison's shopping center works for the law firm that is handling Madison's estate. He told Robert that Monica Madison, Rupert's wife, inherited the whole shebang. She has no interest in running the company, and the kids are still too young. She's going to sell all of it. The shopping center will be, at the very least, on hold until she finds a buyer, and possibly longer if the new owners drop the project. Either way, Higgins will stay on his farm. Boom, motive."

"For both," he suggested.

"Both? I don't follow."

"If Monica Madison was the sole heir to the business fortune that makes her a suspect."

"Except she was in Hawaii."

"Allegedly," he said.

"Ah, see that's why they pay you for this job, and I just get the occasional pat on the back."

"It'll be easy enough to check out her alibi. Anything else?"

Edward had bored waiting for me to get off the phone. He was like an impatient kid. He picked up three apples from the fruit bowl and started juggling them. It would have been an impressive feat if he wasn't using his ghostly energy to move the fruit around in a Ferris wheel style circle.

"Don't bruise my fruit," I scolded.

"Huh?" Jackson asked.

"Sorry, I'm being treated to the circus clown fruit juggling act. I ate lunch at Emily's and dropped by home to check on Sassy and Coco. I have one more thing that might be relevant. Robert Higgins was an avid hunter until a bad knee put an end to it. It stands to reason, he knows how to shoot a target. And now, on to something bigger."

"There's more. Jeez, you really should be getting more than a pat on the back for this."

"Maybe you could mention something to the chief," I suggested facetiously. Any mention of my involvement on murder cases would probably get Jackson demoted or fired. "When I got to Emily's house, Felicity Rossdale was there buying eggs for a birthday cake."

"I had a message from her but haven't had time to call her. What did she say? Did she remember who bought the suitcase?"

"She remembers a young woman who was planning a trip to a spiritual retreat and needed a suitcase. She was wearing dark sunglasses, so Felicity didn't see much of her face, but she said the woman was wearing a big pink crystal around her neck. I just happen to have a good friend who might know something about pink crystals and spiritual retreats. I'm going to head over to Raine's right after I check on the goats. I'll let you know if she adds anything, like a name."

"Great. I'm going to head over to the Higgins Farm and have a chat with Robert. And, I have a Hawaiian alibi to check out. See you later and stay cool."

"I'm always cool," I said. "Oh, wait, you mean in the literal sense. Little chance of that. Later."

I dreaded the idea of leaving the coolness of the house, but I stepped out into the backyard. Even the insects had found it too hot. The tall summer grass was motionless with not even a gentle breeze to give it a push. The girls, as I called them, were inside their shelter resting like Higgins' cows in the shade.

Sassy bleated weakly to let me know it was far too hot for a proper greeting. I checked their water and tossed in a handful of their favorite grain. They were too hot to bother with it. "I'm with you, girls. It's even too hot for treats."

I headed back to the Jeep. The interior was even hotter than a few minutes earlier when I drove home from Emily's. Touching the steering wheel took fortitude and a clever hand dance to keep my palms from burning.

The inside of the Jeep was just getting to a comfortable, cool temperature when I reached Raine's house. That meant I'd have to stop the motor, open the door and start the whole cycle over again.

Raine had figured out the perfect way to deal with the heat. She'd dragged her plastic kiddie pool out for an afternoon splash. She was sitting in her swimsuit, sunglasses and wide-brimmed hat, leaning against the side of the pool with a glass of tea in her hand. Her bare feet rested on the other side of the pool. A hose kept cool water circulating around her.

I stood over her with hands on hips. "You, my friend, know how to deal with a heatwave."

"I may stay in here for the rest of the day. The house is too hot for tea leaves and incense. I cancelled the rest of my appointments. I'd invite you in, but there's no room, and I'm not entirely sure this pool can support two of us." She lifted her sunglasses and squinted. "You look—let me see—what's the word—"

"Bedraggled?" I asked.

"Good one. I guess that's why you get paid for your words. What brings you to my neck of the woods?" She sat forward quickly enough to send waves over the short side of the pool. "Did I forget a lunch date or something?"

"Nope. I'm hoping you can help with the Madison case."

"Seriously? How can I help?" She relaxed back with her tea.

"Do you know a young woman, brown hair, who wears a big pink crystal around her neck for positive energy and who has plans to attend a spiritual retreat?"

Raine rolled her eyes before replacing her sunglasses. I could see my reflection in the shiny, dark lenses. Bedraggled was spot on.

"That would be Shelby Arthur. She fancies herself a budding spiritualist and tarot card reader. She hangs onto that pink crystal like a baby hangs onto its pacifier."

I took out my phone and typed the name into my reminders. "I take it by the condescending tone; the two of you aren't friends."

A laugh rolled from her mouth. With the sunglasses, hat and glass of tea she reminded me of an old-time movie star floating in her pool and sipping mint juleps.

"We're not friends, and as far as her sixth sense goes, she might be able to predict the weather after looking at the weather app."

"Ouch, that was catty."

"I suppose so. It's the heat. Besides that, I'm feeling rather Greta Garbo-ish in my swimming pool and get-up."

I shook my head. "Sometimes you scare me. You read my mind. I didn't put the Garbo label on it but it works."

"See, that's a sixth sense. Shelby has a five-and-a-half sense, if that."

"A five-and-a-half sense?" I asked.

"Yes. Just made that up. Anyhow, did she kill Madison? Never pegged her as a killer. Only a wannabe."

"My, someone really has gotten into the movie star mode. I don't think she did it, but she might be connected. Do you know where she lives?"

"Not really. I think she used to rent a condo somewhere. She worked at the candle shop, but last time I was there she wasn't working. There was a new manager."

Standing over the pool, watching the cold water flow from the hose, was making me feel even hotter. "I'm going to let you get back to your swim, Greta."

"Did I help?" she asked.

"Definitely. See you later. Don't get too pruned."

"Too late. If you get too hot, I'll let you put your feet in later," she called as I headed back to the Jeep. I pulled out my phone and texted Jackson. "I've got a name. Shelby Arthur."

"Thanks. I'll buy you an ice cream for payment. Meet me at the park in twenty?"

"Yes."

"Chocolate shell or no chocolate shell?" he texted back.

"Do you really have to ask?" I said in return.

CHAPTER 30

*J*ackson was sitting on one of the picnic tables gently holding two chocolate coated soft-serve ice cream cones. He'd been working on his treat already. Most of the shell was gone.

He handed a cone to me. "Better hurry before it melts into a chocolate puddle."

I immediately removed a large section of chocolate. It melted in my mouth. "Hmm, these always remind me of summer as a kid. My dad would walk us down the road to the ice cream shop in the evenings. I always got soft-serve vanilla with a chocolate shell. Lana was more daring. She'd get one of the new flavors like pistachio or white chocolate chip. And Emily always got the orange sherbet. I'm surprised you had time to stop for ice cream since you're doubled up."

Jackson had his ice cream down to the cone. "That's why I stopped for ice cream. It was a reward for doing two jobs. I never hear thanks from the captain or chief about having to take over two cases, so I decided to reward myself. They always expect it without giving it another thought. Kind of annoying."

"They're taking you for granted. Any word from Willow?"

"I called Roy earlier to let him know we got a signed confession on his case. He tried to sound cheery, but it was obvious he was in pain. A little slurry with his words too, so at least the pain pills have kicked in. I'm not expecting him back anytime soon." He took a bite of his cone. Bits of it fell on the ground. A pigeon swooped in out of seemingly thin air to clean up after him.

"Did you find out anything about Monica Madison? I still can't believe it didn't at least occur to me that she might have killed her husband to inherit his fortune. They were estranged, after all. I'd heard she was living in Hawaii with her kids, so the notion never even took hold. It seems I forgot there were these big, modern inventions called airplanes that could transport someone across the world in less than a day."

"Don't beat yourself up about it too much. I checked out the story. Monica Madison and her two children arrived from Honolulu Wednesday morning, after they learned of Madison's death. So, she's off the list."

"And Robert Higgins?" I asked.

"I stopped by his farm. You're right. He is no longer selling the place. He insists he was in bed by eight on Tuesday night. He gets up at the crack of dawn to feed and water the animals." Jackson looked over at me. "We're not going to be *those* kind of farmers, are we? The crack of dawn sounds painful. Not too bad now when it's too hot to sleep, but in the dead of winter, no thanks."

"I agree. We'll have to train the animals to follow a more reasonable feeding schedule. What's your sense?" I returned to the case. "Did Higgins kill Madison?"

"He was definitely nervous during the interview but then that sometimes happens naturally with people. The badge tends to make people bunch up into a pile of taut nerves."

"He was cool as a cucumber with me," I said. "Invited me in for tea and everything."

Jackson finished the last bite of cone. I handed him the rest of mine.

"Are you sure?" he asked.

"The chocolate is gone. The rest are just the parts that held up the chocolate."

He dragged his tongue around the swirly mountain of ice cream. Thick white drips flowed down the cone. He took a big bite to get ahead of the melt, then pressed his hand against his forehead. "Ouch. Too much at once. Back to the conversation," he said, "you blithely entered the house of a possible killer for a glass of tea?"

I blinked at him. "There were lemon slices. Your point?"

He shook his head. "You know what my point it, Sunni, because I make the same point at least once a month. It's dangerous."

"Is there anything that seems remotely dangerous about Robert Higgins?"

"Not particularly." Jackson pulled a napkin from his pocket and wrapped it around the quickly disintegrating ice cream cone. "But I've arrested silver-haired, little old ladies for murder."

"You keep using that poor old woman, Mrs. Kelly, as a reason for me to be afraid of every possible suspect."

"The woman bludgeoned her husband with a frying pan and then attempted to cut up his remains with a butter knife."

"That was a particularly notable murder case," I admitted. "It also sounded like the old guy had it coming with his constant complaints about her cooking."

"Remind me not to mention when something doesn't have enough salt or is a little raw." Jackson finished the ice cream part of the cone. The sun had helped. The ground beneath our feet was dotted with thick white drops of ice cream. A squirrel sat in a nearby tree waiting patiently for us to walk away. Jackson's phone buzzed. He wiped his hands again and pulled it out. "It's the address for Shelby Arthur. I'm heading over to talk to her about the suitcase. Interested in coming?"

"Of course I am." I reached up and dabbed a little ice cream from his stubble-covered chin with my finger. "I've got hand wipes in my car, so you'll be a little less sticky when you inform the woman her yard sale purchase was used in a murder."

CHAPTER 31

I followed Detective Jackson to the next stop in the investigation, the Greenhill Condominium Complex on the far edge of town. It was a two-story complex of light blue condos. The window air-conditioners were buzzing loudly in many of the windows, and a group of teens were playing in the pool.

"We might have had the end-of-summer event, but summer is still in full swing," Jackson noted as we met in the visitor parking section of the lot.

"When I went to see Raine to get the name of the woman with the pink crystal, she was in her kiddie pool sipping iced tea. She told me she planned to stay there all day."

"Maybe we should forget the farm and put in a pool," Jackson suggested.

"You only say that because you are looking for an excuse to rent a big earth mover."

Jackson smiled. "That might be part of the motive." He reached over and flicked open the latch on the gate between the parking lot and the condos. Shelby's condo was on the second floor at the end of a corridor.

He knocked. A voice inside said, "coming."

Shelby Arthur was thirty-something with a deep tan. Her long hair was parted and plaited into dozens of small braids. She was wearing a purple sundress. The pink crystal was even bigger than I expected. It seemed like an unwieldy piece of jewelry to wear all the time.

"Hello, I thought you were my friend." She fingered the crystal absently. "Can I help you?"

Jackson lifted his badge. "I'm Detective Jackson, and this is my assistant Miss Taylor. I wonder if we could come inside. I have a few questions."

She looked hesitant, but it didn't seem from guilt, only about letting two complete strangers into her home. "A detective," she said as fingered the crystal again. "Please, come in. Has something happened?" she asked as she stepped aside.

The décor of the condo was low-key bohemian with silk scarves draped over lamp shades and a futon with a tie-dyed cover for sitting. My nose told me she liked to burn the same collection of candles and incense as Raine.

"What's going on?" she asked. "Is someone in trouble?"

I glanced casually around the room while Jackson explained his reason for our visit. A pair of large sneakers that would definitely not fit Shelby's feet sat on the floor next to the futon.

"We have some questions about a purchase you made at a local yard sale," Jackson started. His first sentence made her eyes round. I couldn't blame her. He made it sound as if yard sale shopping was an illegal offense. I was blaming it on him being overworked and overheated.

"My goodness, I've been shopping at yard sales for years," Shelby said. "I buy stuff all the time." She waved her hand at a lamp that had a giraffe base and a paisley print lampshade. "I bought that two weeks ago at a flea market. The television stand came from a local thrift shop. If I purchased stolen items, I had no idea. I promise." She was talking fast, like a twittering bird.

"There's no problem with your yard sale purchases." Jackson was able to step in once she stopped to take a breath. "We're interested in a suitcase you purchased last weekend at a yard sale on Franklin Road. It's light blue with travel stickers."

She was gripping the pink crystal, apparently hoping to hang on to a lot of positive energy. "I did buy a light blue suitcase. I haven't used it yet. I'm leaving for a retreat on Saturday morning. Does the woman want it back? I'm happy to get a refund. I only paid ten dollars for it." She was either a good actress, or she was completely clueless about what had been inside the suitcase. I was sure it was the latter.

"The owner of the suitcase didn't realize her husband was storing his handgun inside of it for safekeeping." An eye roll would have gone nicely with his comment, but he kept it professional. Granted, it was a highly unusual and not well-thought-out place to hide a gun.

"A gun?" she said with a good dose of shock. "I would never keep a gun. They are pure negative energy. I focus on keeping only positive vibes around me. If there's a gun in that suitcase, I will gladly hand the whole thing over. I don't even need a refund. Just a second." She hurried off on bare feet to the bedroom before Jackson could explain that the gun had been found. She returned moments later with the suitcase. She held it far away from her body as if it contained a bomb or some kind of plague. Her hand was shaking as she handed it off to Jackson. The suitcase had seen better days. It was dented on one corner, and most of the travel stickers had been scratched off leaving behind only the sticky glue, which had, in turn, collected a lot of dust.

"Miss Arthur, we have the gun in evidence. I'm hoping you can help us find out how it got from the suitcase to a murder."

That was the final bad energy Shelby could bear. "A murder?" Her face lost color.

I rushed to her side. "Here, let's get you to the futon."

Shelby let me lead her to her futon. She dropped down as if her legs gave out halfway.

Jackson placed the suitcase down and proceeded to open it.

"You're going to open it here?" Shelby asked with alarm.

"I'm expecting an empty suitcase," Jackson said. "Unless there's something you're not telling us."

She shook her body a little. "Nothing at all. Like I said, I haven't even opened the thing. I should have known that case came with some bad karma. I had a terrible time getting it home on my bicycle. Nearly fell over once. If I hadn't needed it for my retreat, I would have left it on the side of the road. Now, I wish I had. To think it was sitting with its deadly contents in my condo. I'm going to have to burn some sage to clear away the dark energy."

Jackson was holding back a smile. She was definitely entertaining in a charming sort of way, and unless she was an Oscar caliber actress, it was easy to conclude she had nothing to do with the murder.

Jackson lifted the side of the suitcase. Aside from an old boarding pass and a travel-sized tube of toothpaste, it was empty. He searched each pocket like he might search a suspect. He picked up the boarding pass and read it. "This is 15 years old."

Shelby sighed loudly. "Thank goodness. It would take me weeks to get the bad energy out of here. Are you sure you have the right suitcase?" she asked.

Jackson pushed to his feet. "Does anyone else live here?"

"I'm alone," she said quietly.

"Whose shoes are those?" Jackson pointed to the large athletic shoes.

Shelby's bottom lip trembled. "Those belong to Sam, my ex-boyfriend. He said he'd be by today to pick them up and give me back my key." Her voice wavered, and she fanned her hand in front of her face to dry tears. "I'm sorry. We just broke up, so the emotions are still raw." She clutched her pink crystal again. And darn, if holding the rock didn't calm her down. She closed her eyes and took a deep Zen-style breath.

"He's handing back the key?" Jackson started. Her lashes fluttered over her eyes. She was keeping back tears again. "I'm sorry if this is painful, but it's important. Did anyone else have access to that suitcase?"

The color had returned to her cheeks. "I suppose Sam had access. I brought it home the Saturday before last. Yesterday morning was our last big fight. He complained about the smell of the incense. He said it was giving him a headache." Her voice wavered again. She was certainly a delicate flower. "That was when I told him we were through. I couldn't take his constant negativity. I always try to stay positive."

"Yes, you mentioned that." Jackson was not in the mood for her theatrics anymore. "What is your boyfriend's full name and contact information?" He pulled out his notebook. It was easy to predict what would come next.

Not just her bottom lip trembled but her entire chin. "You can't possibly think Sam did it? He sometimes carries around too much negative energy, but he'd never kill anyone."

"Does he have any experience with guns?" Jackson was ignoring her protestations and getting straight to it.

"I don't think so. I hope not. I never would have dated him." Her braids ruffled back and forth like those shell curtains people used to hang in doorways to be hip. "He never talked about guns." She seemed to be freaking out as she questioned her entire relationship. "Maybe he *did* know how to shoot, but he didn't tell me because he knew I'd break up with him."

"Does Sam have any connection to Rupert Madison?" Jackson asked.

"Rupert who?" Shelby was sitting on the front of her futon. She gripped the edges as if it might roll out from under her. The whole discussion was causing her such anxiety, she'd even forgotten about her pink crystal. "I've never heard of him, but Sam and I didn't always discuss everything. We both liked our independence."

An obvious question popped into my head. "How long were you two together?"

Shelby gave it some thought. With the time she took, I expected an answer like four or five years. That's not what I got.

"Next Saturday would have been our three-month anniversary." She wiped at a stray tear. Her emotions were *raw* about a three-month relationship. The poor woman had her work cut out for her in the long roller coaster of life.

"Sam's last name?" Jackson asked.

They'd known each other for a such a short amount of time it took her a second to remember it. "It's Rand—uh—Randall. Yes, that's it. Samuel Randall," she said with newfound confidence. Then, a child-like pout appeared. "Don't tell him I told you. I don't want to be a tattle-tell."

"I don't think it's considered ratting someone out when you just give out their name." The warm, stuffy condo and the somewhat silly interviewee had shortened Jackson's fuse. "Do you happen to know where Sam was on Tuesday night between the hours of 7 and 10 p.m.?"

"This Tuesday?" she asked.

"Yes, two days ago," he added impatiently. Sweat was beading on his forehead. He wanted to get this over with. Even though nothing was burning at that moment, the aroma of incense and candles wafted around the room in a pungent cloud. Raine had that same semi-rancid, flowery odor in her house.

Shelby had to think about it. Raine was right. She didn't have a sixth sense. At this point, even the five-and-a-half-sense suggestion was being generous.

"That's right. I can't believe I forgot. It was my Mom's birthday. We were at her house eating cake and ice cream. We got back here about eleven."

"He was with you the whole time?" Jackson asked. I could see his posture wilting. It seemed his next possible suspect had an alibi.

"Yes, of course. He stepped into the basement to play pool with my brothers for an hour, but he was with me the whole night."

"I'll need your mom's number and Sam's too."

Shelby got up from the futon. "My mom will be worried when she hears from a detective," she said as she walked to the kitchen. She opened a drawer and pulled out a notepad and pen.

"I'll make sure I don't alarm her."

Shelby ripped the paper off and handed it to Jackson. "Sam's a good guy, really. I mean, we didn't make it, but I can vouch for him. He works hard. He's a tree trimmer with Swank Tree Trimming. He expects to be a foreman soon."

Jackson tucked the paper into his pocket. "I'm going to need to take the suitcase, but we can return it once the investigation is over."

"No, please take it, and don't bring it back. I've got a duffle bag that'll work just fine for my trip." She walked us to the door.

"Thanks for your time," Jackson said. His long legs took big steps. "I couldn't breathe in that hot, stuffy room," he muttered. "Might as well have been wearing a ski parka." He put the suitcase in the back of his car.

"I'm sorry that didn't pan out like we thought," I said. "I was sure we were at the end of the road after finding the suitcase. Do you think Sam had something to do with it?"

"Not if the alibi checks out. But I'm going to talk to him—" His phone rang. He released a frustrated sigh as he pulled it out of his pocket. "Jackson here. Right. Text me the address. I'm on my way." Another sigh followed, only it was more of a grunt. "Another dead body. What is going on in this town?" He leaned forward and kissed my forehead. It was far too hot for an embrace. "See you later, Bluebird."

"Hydrate," I reminded him as I headed toward the Jeep.

CHAPTER 32

As hot and sticky as it was, I felt energized. The week had started terribly between Jackson and me, but things had smoothed out again. Now he was being run ragged by the constant demand of his time, and no second detective to help out. I needed to step in and solve Rupert Madison's murder. There was one major suspect I hadn't spoken to yet—Curtis Lang. The first time I tried, I was rudely shooed away by one of his employees. The man had mentioned that Lang spent his day traveling between worksites. I was hoping the triple-digit temperatures would have coaxed him back to the comfort of his office. Given the chance, I would much rather be in the comfort of my home than out on the road, but I had a job to do. Not a journalist job. My other job—as Detective Jackson's *assistant*.

I drove to the industrial complex that housed Lang Construction. I parked the Jeep. It seemed I was in luck. I could see a tall, lean man with a tan and graying sideburns walking toward a desk in the office. So far, I'd only seen Curtis's son, Kyle. He'd shyly approached Lauren at the summer fair. It made sense that the man sitting in the small office was the owner of the company, Curtis Lang.

I wondered if I'd get the same rude treatment. I pulled open the glass door and stepped inside. A wall air conditioning unit was running full tilt and churning out the noise to go with it. The man I'd seen through the window looked leathery up close. He was handsome beneath the tanned wrinkles. His smile only added to his looks. "How can I help you?" he asked.

I lifted my press pass almost begrudgingly. I could have made up a lie about considering a building project, only the heat had sapped me of my creative energy. I couldn't come up with a good enough story on such short notice.

He squinted to read my pass. "Sunni Taylor with the *Junction Times*. I'm Curtis Lang. How can I help you?"

"I am in the middle of writing an article about the Madison shopping center project. The newspaper owner, Prudence Mortimer, gave me the assignment." I'd found that name-dropping the newspaper's owner sometimes opened the door for me, especially with people like Curtis Lang, who probably spent his time closer to Prue's social circles than to mine.

"Yes, I heard Mrs. Mortimer bought the paper. Good for her. Lang Construction built a large custom gazebo in her backyard."

"That was yours? It's wonderful."

"Thank you. She invited a garden magazine to come take pictures of it." The pleasantries over, he shifted to a more formal expression. "I'm afraid you've come to the wrong person about the Madison shopping center. My company is not involved in the project. In addition"–his mouth flattened to a grim line—"I'm sure you've heard about the tragic death of Rupert Madison."

"I have. I was at movie night. Were you there? It was so shocking."

"I was home with my wife. She doesn't care for big social events. They give her anxiety." I didn't want to throw a wrench into our discussion by suddenly going all police-ish asking if his wife could corroborate that and were they together the whole night. (I was itching to ask those questions.)

"I'd heard your company had an interest in building the shopping center. But you said you're not involved with it?"

"That's right. I put in a bid to build it, but Madison had another company lined up for the job."

"I'll bet that was disappointing," I said.

He shrugged. "As they say—you win some, you lose some. It would've been silly for me not to put in a bid. My company is local, and we've built shopping centers and neighborhoods. We have the resources and talent for a big project. Madison liked to cut corners. He *really* liked to cut corners," he repeated. The last was more to himself.

"I've heard that about him. There's an angry group of homeowners suing his company because of shoddy workmanship. I assume your company had nothing to do with that."

His demeanor had been pleasant and relaxed right up to the last part. He fidgeted with a few papers on his desk. "That group of disgruntled homeowners is being led by a woman Rupert used to date. She had her heart broken, so she was trying to make his life miserable. I wouldn't be surprised if it turned out she shot Rupert."

"You're talking about Veronica Blaine?"

He looked up from his desk. "Then you know her. Those houses are long past their warranty, so she doesn't have a legal leg to stand on. I'm sure she'll be dropping her lawsuit soon enough now that the real reason behind it, Rupert Madison, is dead."

"She sent me a list of problems the homeowners were having. There were some pretty big issues, especially considering the houses are only three years old."

"Look, Madison was all about profit. I suppose it doesn't hurt to say that now. He should have taken more pride in his projects, but it was always about money. As a contractor, I was obligated to follow his orders. Occasionally, we got into an argument about it, but I wanted to get the houses finished and be done with it."

"It's surprising, then, that you considered working for him again on a big shopping center."

His nostrils widened. It seemed I'd be shooed away soon enough. "It's not the same when you build a shopping center. People don't live in the shops, scrutinizing every issue. They're mostly vacant spaces with little detail. In this industry, landing a shopping center is a big prize. No disgruntled homeowners to deal with afterward."

"Then, not getting the contract must have been upsetting."

He stared up at me. "As I said, it's part of the business. If I never put together quotes, I'd have no business. If you don't mind, Miss Taylor, this interview is over. I have work to finish."

"Yes, of course. Thanks for your time." Hot, sticky air blasted me as I stepped back outside. I didn't get any sense that Curtis was angered about being turned down for the shopping center, but he certainly got his hackles up when I brought up the homeowner lawsuit. I wasn't so sure that legal mess was over, and while he didn't confirm it, I was sure the Lang Company was part of the lawsuit.

There were still some hours in the day. I'd noticed a Swank Tree Trimming truck off Crimson Grove on my way to Lang's office. With any luck, Sam Randall was working at the site.

CHAPTER 33

Crimson Grove was lined with some of the area's most beautiful sugar maple trees. In the fall, the road which connected the heart of Firefly Junction to the Colonial Bridge was so ripe with color, people flocked there to take pictures. Today, the trees were still summer green. But, if you looked closely, you saw some edges of autumn creeping into the foliage as the trees shut down for the dormant season. Three Swank Tree Trimming trucks were parked on the side of the road, including the big, loud truck chewing up debris like the world's scariest shark and spitting it out as mulch.

No trees were being chopped down, but the Crimson Grove sugar maples were getting a much-needed haircut. The county sent in crews once a year to keep the branches from getting tangled in electrical wires. Two workers were suited up in bright orange vests to control traffic and divert cars around the work area. Two tree trimmers were dangling in harnesses inside the trees hacking away at the maze of branches with their chainsaws. Other workers bundled the falling debris and fed it into the *tree chewer*. There was only one woman on the crew. She was holding the stop sign at the other end of the work area. I had no idea what Samuel Randall looked like, but I assumed he'd be in his thirties like Shelby. It was hard to see faces under the hardhats, safety goggles and ear protection, but a few of the men looked more *weathered* than others. The one holding the stop sign on my side of traffic looked incredibly young, like just out of high school young.

Bright orange cones had been set up around the work area, and I found myself in line between cars waiting to be ushered forward while the opposite side of traffic was waved through. The delay worked in my favor. My Jeep ended up right next to the young crew member. I rolled down my window. "Excuse me," I said.

He was hesitant to talk to me. He glanced around, seemingly for his supervisor, then leaned forward. "It should only be another five minutes. We go on break after that."

"Right. Good to know." It was very good to know.

"Is Samuel Randall here this morning? I don't see him, and I need to talk to him."

"Sam? Yeah, he's up in the tree. He's coming down right now in fact."

I stretched up to see past the big mulching truck. One of the harnessed men was lowering himself down with a pulley. His chainsaw dangled from his right arm.

"Thanks," I told the kid and rolled up my window. The tree chewer was still screaming like a hundred cats that had their tails stepped on all at once. It was finally our turn to drive through. I stopped the Jeep well past the worksite and waited a few minutes for thermoses, coffee cups and wrapped sandwiches to come out. Everyone looked the same in their bright orange protective vests and hardhats, but Samuel was taller than the rest. I kept an eye on him in my rearview mirror. He stepped out of his harness, lowered the ear protection to his neck and pulled his goggles and hat off to eat a sandwich on the side of the road a few feet away from the trucks.

I got out of the Jeep. Now that the traffic signs had been put down, cars flowed in both directions until the buildup on both sides was gone. Crimson Grove was generally a quiet road. Once the last car had gone through, I crossed the street to where Samuel was standing and eating a sandwich.

"Mr. Randall?"

Sam looked up from his sandwich. There was a clean line above where his helmet had sat, but a fine layer of dirt covered the rest of his face and the backs of his hands. He was using a paper towel to hold the sandwich.

"Yes?"

"I'm Sunni Taylor with the *Junction Times*."

"You probably want my supervisor, Bob. He's the guy with the gray hair and yellow vest."

"Actually, it's you I was hoping to talk to. I've been writing about the Rupert Madison murder."

His brows hopped up to the clean hat line. "Don't know how I can help you with that."

"Well, it's a long, somewhat convoluted story. Did you know the man?"

He shook his head. "Only through what I've heard about him. He was kind of a hardheaded man to work for. At least, that's what I've heard. We don't have that problem here. Swank, the owner, treats us all well with good pay and benefits."

"That's always good to hear. I'll get to the point. I know you're on break. Your girlfriend—"

"Ex-girlfriend," he corrected. "Shelby and I broke up. Best for both of us. She was getting deep into this psychic stuff. She's convinced she'll be able to talk to the spirit world one day." He laughed. "Can you imagine anything so crazy?"

I laughed lightly. "Never in a million years. This is about a suitcase Shelby bought at a yard sale."

His entire expression changed. The amusement was gone. "Yeah, I know about the suitcase." He squinted at me. "What about it?" It seemed I'd found the person who'd opened the suitcase and discovered the gun. The question now was—what did he do with that gun? If he didn't know Madison, it seemed unlikely he would have killed the man.

"The woman who sold it to Shelby didn't realize that her husband was storing his gun inside the suitcase, a Glock 19. Did you happen to open the suitcase?"

"Maybe. What does this have to do with Madison's murder?" Samuel was putting the pieces together.

There was no reason to sugarcoat it. "The gun was used in the murder."

Samuel stepped back as if someone had struck him. "Jeez, I didn't know someone would use it to kill Madison. Shelby asked me to put the suitcase in her closet. As I was pushing it inside, something hard knocked around. I opened it and found the gun. It was a little shocking to see. I didn't tell Shelby because she would have freaked out and run around the condo burning smelly herbs to rid the place of bad karma." In three months, he'd gotten to know the woman pretty well. "I probably should have turned it into the police or given it back to the people who sold the suitcase, but I needed the money. I took it to a pawn shop and sold it. I didn't know someone would buy it to kill Rupert Madison."

"Which pawn shop?" I asked.

"The one on Bear Road near Smithville. The guy specializes in guns. I'm sorry it happened, but I assure you I had nothing to do with the murder. That gun was in my possession maybe three hours. I didn't want anything to do with it. Just needed some cash. I'm working on a '65 Mustang, and they had some parts I needed at the car salvage yard."

A whistle blew letting the crew know it was time to start work again.

Samuel stared at his half-eaten sandwich.

"Gosh, I'm sorry you didn't get a chance to finish that."

Sam shrugged. "This? I can gobble it down in two bites. Do you think I'll have the cops coming around to ask me about the gun? I mean, you're just a reporter, and you knew about it."

I smiled. "Well, I might be *just* a reporter, but sometimes, we know things long before the cops. And yes, you might have a visit from someone in the department. Just tell them what you told me."

The loud mulch truck fired up again. That was my cue to leave. I hurried across before the traffic controllers picked up their signs. I climbed into the Jeep. The natural shade from the trees had helped keep the interior from heating up like a furnace. I looked up the name and address of the pawn shop near Smithville, then I sent a text to Jackson.

"Samuel Randall had the gun in his possession for a short amount of time. He sold it to Bear Road Pawn Shop. I'm heading there now to see if I can find out who bought it. I think I'm getting closer."

CHAPTER 34

The Bear Road Pawn Shop was on its own quiet corner past a gas station and before a small strip mall with a shoe repair shop, a pharmacy and a pet supply store. It was a small building with cedar siding. Bars covered the three front windows and the window on the front door. The flashing neon sign on top of the building said *Guns, Antiques and Jewelry*.

I parked the Jeep, slipped my press pass under my shirt and got out. Late afternoon was finally bringing a reprieve from the sweltering temperatures. A bell clanged as I swung open the door. A window air conditioner was blowing around mostly hot air. Two women were looking at a Victorian era settee. A man with short brown hair brushed to the side and a white shirt with rolled-up sleeves stood behind the counter cleaning some old jewelry.

"Let me know if there's anything behind glass that you'd like to see."

I headed toward the counter as he spoke. Several locked glass cabinets lined the wall behind the counter. They were filled with guns of every shape and size. "Are you looking for a gun?" he asked.

"I'm looking for a particular gun. I'm out of ideas, so I hope you can help me. My husband had been storing his personal handgun, a Glock 19, in an old suitcase. I didn't realize it was in there, and I sold the suitcase at a yard sale. I recovered the suitcase, but the gun was gone. I'm hoping to find it before my husband realizes the mistake I've made. By any chance, did someone come in here last week to pawn a Glock 19?"

His brows lowered sympathetically. "I did have a young man sell me a Glock 19 last week."

I needed to make sure it was the right gun. "Was he in his thirties, possibly covered in tree debris?"

"He was wearing a t-shirt with the Swank logo." The sympathetic expression grew sharper. "I thought you didn't know who had the gun?"

I paused to rearrange the lies piled in my head. "Like I said, I recovered the suitcase. A woman who lived down the road from me bought it, and since it was missing, she assumed her ex-boyfriend took the gun. She's the one who suggested I try pawn shops because she knew he needed money." I had to keep up the ruse. "I'll pay whatever price is on it. I really need to get that gun back."

"I'm sorry but that Glock's gone. It was the oddest thing. The man who sold it to me came in with a guy he kept calling Cuz, which I assume was short for cousin. That cousin came back here on Monday afternoon to buy the gun."

I nearly pitched forward in excitement. "Did you get a name?"

His cheeks rounded. "I can't give out that kind of information."

"Are you sure? My husband is going to be so disappointed when I tell him. I'd offer the guy good money to buy it back."

The two women approached the counter. "We'd like to buy the settee," one woman said. "Do you deliver?"

"No ma'am, we're a pawn shop. Not a furniture store. Maybe you could rent a truck," he suggested.

"I'll have to arrange something," she said with an aggravated sigh. "Can I leave a deposit?"

"You can, but if someone comes in with the whole amount ready to go, I'll have to sell it to them and refund your deposit. Again, this isn't a furniture store. Cash is preferable."

"Fine. We'll be back." The two women took one more look at the settee and hurried out.

"That settee has been sitting there for six months, but I know how this place works. If one person suddenly wants it, then I'll have at least three more people come in to ask about that Victorian settee. Always happens."

I stood at the counter nodding along and adding my most friendly smile.

"That's right. You wanted the name of the customer who bought the Glock. I'll give the name but no contact information, all right?"

"Absolutely."

He reached under the counter and pulled out a large binder. He flipped through a few pages, ran his finger down a line of names and looked up. "His name is Jeremy, Jeremy Sexton." He shut the book promptly. "Hope that helps. You know, I have a lot of nice guns in the cases. Maybe you'd rather just buy a new one."

"No, this one was special. His grandfather bought it for him." Sometimes the lies came so easily I scared myself.

"That's fine. Anything else I can show you?" He waved his hand toward the pile of jewelry sitting on the countertop.

"No, I have what I need." I turned and walked out of the store. My phone was out of my pocket before I got to the Jeep.

This time I *called* Jackson. It went straight to voicemail. Jackson must have been deep in a crime scene. Poor guy. He was already exhausted and at the end of his tether when we left Shelby's condo.

"Hey, it's me, your super sleuth partner. Jeremy Sexton killed Rupert Madison. He's the young man that Rupert fired because Jeremy's apple core rolled beneath Madison's foot. I guess soaking him in the dunk tank wasn't enough payback. Call me when you get this message, and I'll tell you how I unraveled this. Love you."

I hung up and got into the Jeep. A quick online search didn't get me any closer to finding Jeremy. Evan, the site manager at Sunridge, mentioned he was planning to hire Jeremy back since Rupert was no longer there to give orders. I wondered if he was back at work. There was only one way to find out.

CHAPTER 35

My phone rang while I was on the road. "Hey, Super Sleuth Sunni speaking," I laughed. "Nice alliteration, too. Did you get my message?"

"I did. Where are you now?"

"I'm heading over to the Sunridge Community construction site. The construction manager told me he was going to hire Jeremy Sexton back. I'm hoping he'll be there. Where are you?"

"Heading back to the precinct. They're booking a suspect. But I can tell them to keep him in holding. I'll meet you out there. Don't approach this guy alone. By the way, how did you figure out it was him?"

"It was easy. He's cousins with Samuel Randall, Shelby's ex-boyfriend. Samuel sold the gun to a pawn shop, and Jeremy went there after Madison fired him and bought the gun."

"Sounds like we've got the right guy. Or, I should say, you've got the right guy. Good work as usual, Bluebird. Not sure what I'd do without you."

"You'd be stretched even thinner. Maybe they need to think about hiring a third detective."

His laugh rolled through the phone. "They're on such a tight budget, they told us we had to start bringing our own coffee. It's ridiculous. I'm going to let them know I'm delayed, so I can head out to Sunridge. See you soon, super sleuth."

I laughed. "More alliteration. Bye." I drove straight to the construction site. If Jeremy wasn't there, then I'd wasted Jackson's precious time. But that was all right. I'd already cut short the time required to solve the Madison murder.

I parked in front of one of the many vacant dirt plots at the entrance to the community. They'd already finished one house and had started on two more since my last visit. With at least a dozen workers moving lumber and hammering nails, walls went up fast. I got out of the car and lifted my sunglasses to get a better look at the people working within the frame of the new house. My heart sank when I didn't see Jeremy.

I got out of the Jeep and headed toward the construction zone. As expected, I was stopped before I got within five hundred feet of where the action was happening. Evan had been standing on the front porch of the model home talking on the phone when he spotted me.

"Hey, no one is allowed past the orange cones," he yelled.

I was a foot away from passing them. I turned on my heels and headed toward the model home. Evan recognized me. He hung up his phone. "You're the reporter."

"That's right. I'm looking for Jeremy Sexton. Did he come back to work?"

"I'm back. Who are you?"

I spun around. Jeremy was rolling a wheelbarrow of rubbish to the big bin just past the worksite.

"This is a reporter from *Junction Times*," Evan explained. "She was here the day Madison fired you. She saw the whole thing and gave Madison a piece of her mind about it." Evan was still under the impression I was there to get a quote from

Jeremy, give him support and congratulate him on getting his job back. Maybe that scenario was my best bet. It was certainly better than blurting out the question "did you kill Rupert Madison?"

Evan left the porch. "You've got five minutes, Jeremy, then I need you to pick up the debris on block C."

Jeremy looked more than reluctant to talk to me. His dark eyes seemed to be assessing whether or not talking to a reporter was a good move. I would be doing the same thing if I knew I'd killed a man. "What do you need?" he asked dryly.

"As your supervisor mentioned, I was here the day Rupert fired you. I see you're back, so that's good news."

"That's because I shouldn't have been fired in the first place."

"I couldn't agree more and told Mr. Madison as much right after the incident."

"Appreciate that." A greasy strand of hair fell over his forehead as he nodded. "Look, it's my first day back, and I want to show the boss that he didn't make a mistake rehiring me. I don't know what you want me to say about it. Madison was your typical hardheaded rich man. The apple core was an insult. It hurt his big ego, so he took it out on me. That's all I've got say." His phone rang in his pocket. He pulled it out and answered it before I could ask another question.

"Hey, Sam, I've got two minutes. What do ya need?" He tucked the phone between his head and shoulder, picked up the wheelbarrow and rolled it toward the bin. It was directly across from where I'd parked the Jeep.

It took me a second to realize Sam was Jeremy's tree cutting cousin. Was Sam calling to tell Jeremy about the nosy reporter asking questions about the suitcase gun? I plotted out my best path back to my car. I hurried across the road to make a wide berth around the back of the Jeep. My heart skipped a few beats when Jeremy clumsily and brusquely dropped the wheelbarrow to the ground. He grabbed the phone to hold it better to his ear and glanced around until he spotted me.

"Hey, wait," he yelled and took off toward me.

I got to the passenger side of the Jeep. I climbed inside and locked the doors. Jeremy pounded on the windows. His angry face peered through the glass. "What are you up to?" he yelled. There was so much noise at the construction site; no one seemed to hear the angry man pounding on the Jeep. "I didn't kill him. You don't have any proof."

"You bought the gun that killed him. Pretty sure that's proof."

"That jerk deserved everything he got. He thought he was king, and we were all his servants." Jeremy's face was beet red, and his jaw clenched tightly. He pulled his arm back and made a solid fist. He was going to shoot it like a torpedo through the window. I wasn't entirely sure which would come out on top, his fist or the window, but if he broke through, I'd be in trouble. I reached over and blew the horn as long and as hard as I could. It startled him and his arm dropped. The horn blast grabbed the attention of some of his coworkers. Their loud tools slowed, and they looked in the direction of the Jeep. Evan's face came out of the crowd. He walked toward us with a concerned expression.

Jeremy gave my car one more punch, a lighter one than he'd imagined seconds before. He took off at a run, his long legs carrying him down the road to where the workers' cars were parked.

Jackson's car came into view. He pulled over with a screeching halt. He threw open the door and jumped out with his gun in hand. Jeremy dropped to his knees and put his hands on his head.

I climbed out of the Jeep. Evan caught up to me. "I don't understand," he said. "What did he say to you that caused this?"

"It wasn't my interview. Jeremy Sexton is being arrested for the murder of Rupert Madison."

"My gosh. I had no idea. And I gave him back his job."

All work behind me stopped, and the rest of the crew made its way toward the police action. I'd had enough of the heat, the dusty construction site and the murder investigation. I got back into the Jeep and drove slowly past where Jackson was standing over the suspect. I winked at him as I drove past. He returned a smile.

CHAPTER 36

I pushed the knife through a tomato. Half of it slipped from my grasp, from the cutting board and from the counter. It slapped the floor with a tomato-y explosion.

"Your cooking talent knows no bounds," Edward drawled from the hearth.

I grabbed a paper towel and set to work cleaning up the mess. "This is my sister's fault for growing such juicy tomatoes." It was Saturday evening after a long week made more grueling by the heat. Detective Willow was back on duty, and Jackson had a much-deserved weekend off. The weather app promised a reprieve from the sweltering triple-digit heat, so Jackson and I had plans for a bike ride and Sunday picnic. Tonight, I'd promised him a home-cooked meal. I'd decided on spaghetti and salad. I even made some of Emily's homemade marinara, which, in my opinion, turned out almost as good as hers. I'd made lemon bars for dessert. They were one of Jackson's favorites. Now, the only thing standing between us and a great weekend was that darn, old elephant.

Jackson and Edward had not been in the same room since last weekend's debacle that ended with Jackson marching out in a huff and Edward spending the next few days confused and hurt and trying to figure out whether or not there was an actual elephant problem. I was feeling anxious about the whole reunion. Both men had promised to try and be more congenial to each other. I wasn't holding my breath.

Redford was the first to hear Jackson's car. The two dogs jumped into their circus act of trying to get to the front door first. Jackson's tone carried through the house as he spoke animatedly to the dogs. They were three best buddies, and the dogs knew they'd been missing their third Musketeer all week.

The three of them stepped into the kitchen. I held my breath as Jackson's gaze swept over to the hearth. "Edward," he said politely.

"Brady," Edward responded.

It was very forced and slightly amusing, but I'd take it.

"I smell oregano and garlic." Jackson took a deep whiff of air. He lifted up a bottle of red wine. "Guess I made the right choice."

"Goody. I was hoping you'd bring something. I'll take a glass now while I'm finishing the salad."

Jackson found the corkscrew and got to work opening the wine.

"Sunni tells me you had a difficult work week," Edward said politely.

"Yes. Three murders in a row and the second detective out with a bad back," Jackson explained calmly.

"That does sound taxing. And the weather didn't cooperate either, I understand."

"It was hot and humid all week," Jackson replied.

"That's a shame."

I spun around. "All right. This is cute, but it's kind of like—kind of like listening to fingernails on a chalkboard, if you know what I mean."

"We're just having a conversation," Jackson said.

"Yes, a perfectly reasonable conversation," Edward agreed.

"Fine. Then carry on." I turned back and chided myself for stepping in. They were making an effort, and as comical as it was, it was better than the alternative. Or was it? Maybe I was the problem? Maybe I was far too involved in their relationship. They were, after all, family. Was I the catalyst? Were they always expecting me to step in to mediate? Was I now, at this moment, overthinking the whole darn thing? Probably.

"Brady, I was looking out at the site for your future barn. Have you taken into consideration drainage? It seems you need to create a slope from the east side, so it'll drain properly. You can't allow your horses to stand in moisture. It ruins their hooves."

I cut my cucumbers. My ears were practically crawling to the back of my head as I waited for Jackson's defensive response. It would be the first spark, and from there, the conversation could take a wildfire-sized turn.

"You know something, Edward, you're right. I'll rent the tractor again and start working on that slope tomorrow."

I smiled as I finished the salad. I knew it wouldn't last, but it sure was nice. Besides that, Jackson would come up with any excuse possible to ride around on a tractor moving dirt back and forth.

Jackson came up behind me, kissed the side of my neck and handed me a glass of wine. Normally, any show of affection from Jackson would set Edward off, but he didn't say a word. I spun around for a real kiss and noticed Edward had vanished. He was giving us privacy.

"What are you smiling at, Bluebird?" Jackson asked as he gazed at me with his smoky amber eyes.

"I'm thinking I've got it pretty darn good."

ABOUT THE AUTHOR

London Lovett is author of the Port Danby, Starfire, Firefly Junction, Frostfall Island and Scottie Ramone Cozy Mystery series. She loves getting caught up in a good mystery and baking delicious, new treats!

Learn more at:
www.londonlovett.com

Printed in Great Britain
by Amazon